THE CHRISTMAS PARTY

BOOKS BY KATHRYN CROFT

The Girl With No Past
The Girl You Lost
While You Were Sleeping
Silent Lies
The Warning
The Suspect
The Lie
The Wedding Guest
The Girl in Room 12
Two Mothers
The Last One to See Him
Sophie Was Here

The Lying Wife
The Neighbour Upstairs
The Other Husband
The Mother's Secret

THE CHRISTMAS PARTY

Kathryn Croft

bookouture

First published as an Audible Original in October 2024 by Audible Ltd. This edition published October 2025 by Bookouture.

An imprint of Storyfire Ltd.
Carmelite House
50 Victoria Embankment
London EC4Y 0DZ

www.bookouture.com

The authorised representative in the EEA is Hachette Ireland
8 Castlecourt Centre
Dublin 15 D15 XTP3
Ireland
(email: info@hbgi.ie)

Copyright © Kathryn Croft, 2024, 2025

Kathryn Croft has asserted her right to be identified as the author of this work.

All rights reserved. No part of this publication may be reproduced, stored in any retrieval system, or transmitted, in any form or by any means, electronic, mechanical, photocopying, recording or otherwise, without the prior written permission of the publishers.

ISBN: 978-1-83618-662-5
eBook ISBN: 978-1-83618-661-8

This book is a work of fiction. Names, characters, businesses, organizations, places and events other than those clearly in the public domain, are either the product of the author's imagination or are used fictitiously. Any resemblance to actual persons, living or dead, events or locales is entirely coincidental.

PROLOGUE
2024

Two months before Christmas

Her silky voice is just as I remember it, yet somehow also unfamiliar, as if it belongs to a stranger.

Gabby Sharp. A name I've pushed to the depths of my mind.

'Sasha, how are you?' she asks. 'It's been a long time, hasn't it.'

For a moment I struggle to form any words, and my hand reaches to end the call. But what good would that do? The past always catches up with us eventually. 'Nearly twelve years,' I say.

'That's precisely why I thought it was about time we all got together. For Christmas. You don't have any plans, do you?' It's more of a command than a question. 'I've already called the others and they're all coming. We should all be together, shouldn't we? It's important.'

She lets that hang between us, and my mind scrambles to make sense of this. Her call has exploded into my life like a bomb. Everything was normal until a few seconds ago. I'd just taken Scratch for a walk and was about to curl up on the sofa with a book. And now that dark shadow I've been running from looms over me. I thought I'd laid those ghosts to rest.

'Everyone's going?' I ask.

'Yes. Including Finley. At first, he said he couldn't, but he soon came around. And the others didn't hesitate.'

I don't dare ask what she'd said to persuade him. Fin. The man I thought I'd end up marrying. Until everything changed.

'Where?' I ask.

'I have a second home in Scotland. A beautiful house overlooking a loch. You'll love it. Even in winter it's spectacular. You must come and see it. I got it in my divorce settlement.'

I look around at my small flat. It's cosy and bright and I love it. It's right near Camden Tube station too, so I can easily get around. I can imagine what Gabby would think of it. She was always driven by material things, and clearly nothing's changed.

'It sounds lovely,' I say. 'I wish I could come. But I'm seeing my mum at Christmas.' A lie. Mum is flying off to Florida with a friend for some winter sunshine, so it will just be me and Scratch alone in my flat. I'm happy with that. Jarred moved out a couple of weeks ago and since then I've relished my own company. Just me and Scratch. Not having to worry every day that Jarred would uncover the truth about me. I'm sure he always sensed there was something off about me, but still I let him into my life, assuming it would fizzle out eventually, like it's done with all the other men I've allowed to get close to me. Fleeting connections. That didn't happen with Jarred, and in the end I had no choice but to push him away.

'This is important,' Gabby says. 'Please.' She pauses. 'I've been in therapy, you know. And my therapist said I need to stop hiding from you all. I need to confront my demons and be able to celebrate Christmas with all of us together. I need closure, Sasha, and this is the only way. It has to be on the anniversary. Please.'

'I, um—'

'Thank you. I'll send you all the details. I've got your email address.' She ends the call without another word, and a cold draught fills my flat. I lean back in my chair and stroke Scratch's silky fur to try and regulate my breathing.

People always told us it wasn't healthy. That we all spent far too much time together, rarely venturing outside the boundaries of our friendship group. No good would come of it, they said – how could relationships with others work when the six of us were so tightly interwoven?

In a way, they were right. Not because close friendships like ours don't work – of course they can – but because with all the baggage we each brought to ours, it never stood a chance.

And now, despite the years that have passed, and as much as I want to help Gabby to heal – I know nothing good can ever come of us all being together again.

ONE
NOW

23 December 2024, 15:57

Dark, heavy clouds loom in the sky as I drive along the steep Applecross Peninsula road, and I'm struck by how remote this place is. The backdrop of rugged mountains and view of the coastline is striking, but it chills me to navigate the narrow single-track road and hairpin bends.

Following Gabby's directions, I finally reach the place where her house should be, yet there is no sign of any house from the road. I'm in the right place; Gabby's directions covered the minutest of details, so I know this is where I'm meant to be, but there's no house. I'm six hundred miles from London, in a secluded and unfamiliar place, and I have no idea what I'm about to face.

Deciding I'll have to pull over and call Gabby, I spot a narrow opening between some birch trees, their bare branches desolate and menacing. I head down it, and there in front of me is a sprawling modern home, raised above a loch that seems to stretch endlessly. It feels like the edge of the world, as if nothing exists beyond it, and I've barely passed a house since I reached Wester Ross.

Much of the house is glass, making it feel as though the loch and views are part of the home. Gabby was right – it truly is beautiful. My breath catches in my throat when I think of us all being together. Gabby claimed that was what she needed, for each one of us to be here, to give her some sense of closure, but now I'm here I'm overcome with the sense that we've been summoned for another reason.

Three cars already sit on the expansive driveway: a Range Rover, a BMW X5 and a dark grey Land Rover. I have no idea which is Gabby's, or who the others belong to, but clearly everyone is doing well for themselves.

Taking a deep breath, I open the door of my Golf and make my way across the tiled patio to the front door. There is a video doorbell – of course there is; no one would live here alone without extra security – and I smooth my hair down before I press it. My gesture surprises me; I focus so much on teaching the kids in my class to value more than outward appearances, but somehow being here has made me self-conscious. And I'm about to see Fin after all these years.

It's a few moments before the door swings open and I'm facing a ghost from my past.

'Hey, you!' Gabby says, pulling me towards her. She gives me an air kiss, then pulls back. 'Wow, you've barely changed.'

We both know she's lying. My hair is now its natural chestnut brown, and shorter than I always wore it at university. Changing my appearance was like shedding the past. And it's worked until now. I'm also thinner than I was; my appetite never fully returned after that Christmas.

Gabby, too, looks different. Her hair, the same colour as mine, is also shorter, and her natural waves float on her shoulders. I remember her spending hours ironing them out with her straighteners, and wonder if she stopped bothering after what happened. Things that once seemed important became inconsequential. She's wearing a high-necked light grey wool midi dress that skims her body, and expensive-looking knee-high boots.

'You got here just in time,' she says. 'There's a snowstorm on the way. We don't usually get them until January but... well... climate change, I suppose.' She shrugs. 'Sorry, I didn't think to check the weather. Let's just pray it doesn't get too bad. Anyway, the guys are all here. Shaun and Andre came up together.' Gabby points to the Range Rover and lowers her voice. 'Shaun's doing really well for himself.' She ushers me inside. 'You should have come with them,' she says. 'Or Finley.'

'No, I like driving.' I don't mention that the thought of being in a car with Shaun, Andre or even Fin for twelve hours was unbearable. At one time it would have been as natural as spending time with Scratch. Now our friendship is an empty grave, waiting to be filled. 'Is Anna here yet?' I ask.

'Nope. You know Anna. She'll turn up when she turns up. In her own time, on her own terms. She'll come, though, I know she will.'

I don't want to question how Gabby can be so certain. Anna will come for the same reason I am here: because, ultimately, we have no other choice. Not when Gabby needs our help.

'Where are your things?' Gabby asks, glancing at my car. 'And I hope you've got a warmer coat than that. This is *Scotland*. Of course, the house is warm – underfloor heating is a godsend – but if you wanted to go for a walk at any point then you'll need to wrap up warmer.'

I have no intention of venturing outside into the wilderness that surrounds Loch View House. 'I've got my weekend bag in the car,' I explain. 'I'll get it later.'

Gabby shrugs. 'Suit yourself. Come in, then.' She pulls me inside and closes the door. And now I am trapped inside this luxurious house, with no clear idea of what I'm really doing here, just a faint suspicion that I'm too afraid to acknowledge. 'Did you bring your gift?'

I nod. The instruction from Gabby had come in an email. There is to be a Secret Santa on Christmas Eve, and she'd insisted it was random. She'd got a friend of hers to email us the names, so even Gabby wouldn't know. And I got Fin.

'I've got mine in the car,' I say. 'I hope it's okay.'

'Whatever it is will be perfect,' Gabby says.

She leads me through a large hallway, where voices drift from one of the rooms. Garlands of eucalyptus, pine cones and fairy lights hang above all the doorways, and there's a larger, snow-flocked one intertwined along the banister leading upstairs. The lounge is through double doors at the end of the hallway, with floor-to-ceiling windows on every side, offering panoramic views of the loch. It's a breath-taking sight, and in the corner of the room is a Christmas tree that must be at least eight foot tall, tastefully decorated in only white, silver and blush pink.

My eyes fall on the three men seated around a coffee table on the far side of the room. They turn to face me, and all of them stand. 'Sasha Hunt,' Shaun says, his blue eyes shining. 'Well, well, well. It's... been a long time.' He walks over to me and wraps his arms around me. He always loved going to the gym, but he's become considerably bulkier since our university days, and his arms feel protective and strong. Perhaps I've just forgotten, but his hair seems darker blond than it was, too.

'Good to see you,' I say, pulling away.

Fin is the next to give me a hug, and having his arms around me, the familiar scent of him, makes me feel as if we are right back there, with all the anticipation that surrounded the two of us. That sense of what we would become. I pull back as quickly as is polite. He still has the power to destabilise me, and I can't let that happen.

Other than the dark stubble on his face, Fin hasn't changed

much, and he stares at me as if he can't believe I'm here. His soft brown hair is still short at the sides and longer on top, taking me right back to the last time I saw him. My face burns and I turn away, glancing at Andre, who hovers behind Fin. He hesitates before giving me a brief hug. Out of all of them, Andre is the one who hasn't changed at all, his black hair and golden-brown skin somehow ageless. 'It's been a long time, Sasha,' he says, and I wonder if any of the others can sense that this is a lie.

Driving up here, I wondered what it would be like to come face to face with Andre again. Andre. Who will never let me forget. 'Hello,' I say. He can hide behind a screen all he wants, but now I'm here he will have to face me. And I know he's the one who's been sending me those messages.

'Isn't this lovely,' Gabby says. 'When Anna gets here, we'll finally all be together again after twelve years. This means so much to me. I know it must be hard for you to be here like this, especially at this time. But you came for me.' She smiles. 'I'm sorry there's a storm on the way – I feel so guilty.'

Shaun rushes over to her and hugs her. 'We'll be fine. And of course we all came when you invited us. We're like family, aren't we?'

Nausea bubbles in my stomach. We *were* like family – the six of us drawn together by some force we could never hope to understand – until one of us did something unspeakable. 'So what made you contact everyone, Gabby?' Shaun asks, lifting a glass. He's already on the wine, and if his past is anything to go by, this won't be a good thing. 'I mean, this particular year. I'm just curious. Did you miss me?'

Gabby laughs, but it sounds forced. 'You wish.' She looks at each of us. 'It was time.'

'Ah, not even a little bit?' Shaun says.

Gabby laughs again, more naturally this time, and places her hand on Shaun's chest. 'You're a married man now, Shauny.

What would your beautiful wife say about that? I've seen her on your Facebook page. What a stunning woman.'

'Yeah, she is,' Shaun says, but he looks away and downs the rest of his drink. There is trouble simmering, and already I long to get in my car and drive home, but we're stuck here till the day after Boxing Day. 'Doesn't stop me reminiscing, though,' Shaun says. 'And have you been stalking me?' Although he smiles, it seems false.

'The past never truly leaves us, does it,' Gabby says.

I wonder how she feels about seeing Shaun again. The two of them had been loved up for the whole time we were at university, so seeing him must stir up emotions for her, even after what happened.

Fin shoots me a glance, but I turn away.

'Anyway,' Gabby continues. 'It's getting late, and you must all be hungry. A feast awaits us in the kitchen. And I made it myself. In case you didn't notice on your way here, there's nowhere to order food from. In fact, nowhere to get anything unless you travel for miles.'

'Doesn't it freak you out, being so isolated here?' Andre asks. 'And I've noticed the Wi-Fi is a bit temperamental.'

'Not at all,' Gabby says. 'I find it comforting. And I've got used to the Wi-Fi. Don't worry, though, I have enough food to last for weeks, so we won't run out even when the snowstorm hits.'

Again, Fin glances at me. 'Snowstorm?'

'I know, I should have warned you, but I've been so busy preparing for Christmas, I didn't think to check the weather. Let's just relax and enjoy ourselves. We never got to celebrate that year, did we. Let's just get to know each other again, and tomorrow evening we'll party and celebrate this festive season. Like we were always supposed to.'

I watch the others. Surely they're thinking the same as me:

how can Gabby throw herself into celebrating like this – with all of us – when Christmas Eve is when her life changed? When all our lives changed?

'Come on, then,' Gabby says. 'And Sasha, you need a drink.'

'Just water for me, thanks. Maybe tomorrow.' I don't tell her that I haven't touched a drop for twelve years. And I never will again.

As we all make our way to the kitchen, I feel a tug on my sleeve. I turn around and Fin puts his hand out to make me wait.

'Are you okay?' he asks. 'I noticed just now you looked a bit... I don't know. When Shaun was talking.'

'I'm fine,' I reply.

'Am I the only one beginning to think this is a bad idea?' Fin continues. 'Gabby seems... I don't know. She said on the phone she needed us to be together for closure so she could move on, but... it doesn't feel that way.'

Fin is echoing my thoughts, and it's a relief to know I'm not the only one thinking this way. 'Why else would she have asked us all here?' he continues. 'It doesn't make any sense. Why now?'

I check to make sure Gabby can't hear us. 'I don't know.'

'But we all came because we'd have felt guilty if we didn't when she said how much she needed us all to be here,' Fin says.

'Anna hasn't come yet,' I point out. 'Maybe she won't turn up.'

'She's on her way, though,' Fin says. 'And it really feels like this can't be a good idea. All of us here together.'

'Why did you come?' I'm asking him this even though I can't explain why I came myself.

'For Gabby. Because the friendship we all had meant something to me. But also because I wanted to see you. I *needed* to see you. You never answered my calls all those years ago. Why?'

'You know why. I couldn't. We had to move on. All of us.'

'What if Gabby's playing games?' Fin says. 'I don't think she's right in the head. I could tell the second we got here. This is not going to end well.'

TWO

NOW

19:35

We sit at the table, tucking into the food that Gabby has made. 'This is delicious, Gabby,' Shaun says, digging into his lobster bisque. 'You always knew how to look after people.'

Gabby's face pales. Shaun hasn't changed then, still speaking before engaging his brain. 'More Prosecco?' Gabby says to no one in particular. She pours herself a glass then offers the bottle to Andre, who so far has barely uttered a word. But I've noticed him watching me when he thinks no one's looking. Andre was always shy around women, yet with Shaun and Fin he was a different person. He had his share of interest from women – his dark golden skin and large green eyes make him an attractive man – but I never saw him actually date anyone. He's private, Fin used to insist. That's all it is.

But now I know that none of us really knew him. The next time he glances at me, I narrow my eyes – a silent warning that I won't be intimidated.

The doorbell chimes and Gabby jumps up. 'Finally, she's here.'

As she leaves the room, we all glance around the table at each other. There's no doubt in my mind that we're all thinking the same thing: will Anna bring the same chaos she always did? Or has her fiery nature been tempered?

The sound of muffled voices drifts from the hallway, and it's a few moments before Anna strides in. Her tanned skin and beach-swept dark hair seem out of place in the middle of this stark winter, but then Anna has always gone against the grain, deliberately most of the time. 'Well, hello,' she says. 'This is...' She lets that thought fizzle out, and makes her way towards me. 'Darling Sasha.' She pulls me into her arms and holds me tightly, as if she doesn't want to let go. 'I never thought *this* would happen, did you?' she whispers, but she doesn't wait for an answer and is moving on to Fin, giving him a briefer hug than the one I just received.

I catch her looking back at me when she greets Shaun.

'Come and eat,' Gabby urges, ushering Anna to the table. 'I've made lasagne, and there's pumpkin pie for dessert. Then I'm sure you could all do with an early night before we start the festivities tomorrow. Scotland's a long way to travel. I really do appreciate this. I know you all think I'm not the most grateful person. But... I'm not that same woman I was when...'

'Yep, early to bed for me,' Anna says, yawning. 'I literally just flew in.'

Should I be grateful or annoyed that she's interrupted Gabby when she might have been about to say something that may shed light on what we're actually doing here?

'Where have you been?' Fin asks Anna.

'Oh, I don't live in the UK,' Anna explains. 'I went travelling after uni and settled in Spain. *Es maravilloso!* I love it there. The people. The culture. Everything about it. I feel free there in a way I never have here.'

'Is that right?' Shaun says. 'Seems to me you were pretty free here, am I right?'

I stare at Shaun, who is still knocking back Prosecco, and I wonder what trouble his loose lips will cause tonight.

'I'm not ashamed that I don't put limits on myself,' Anna says. 'You should try it sometime.' She smiles and lifts her glass. 'Cheers!'

'So, are you seeing anyone special?' Gabby asks.

'Just split up with this woman I was seeing. Met her in Málaga, on a beach. She was sunbathing topless right next to me and...' Anna shrugs and smiles at Shaun. 'You know how it is. Lasted five months and then I met her brother. Let's just say Catalina wasn't very happy.'

'Nothing new with you then,' Andre says, almost under his breath.

'Love you too, honey,' Anna says, blowing him a kiss. 'Now, enough about my sex life – how's everyone else's?'

'Well, I'm divorced, so nothing happening on that front,' Gabby says, glancing at Shaun. 'And let's just say I'm happy this way. Helps me think more clearly. No distractions. Everything's changed for the better since I left Edward.' She flaps her arms. 'And look what I get to keep!'

'Yep, this is a beautiful house,' Anna says. 'And the view of the lake must be stunning in daylight.'

'Loch, you mean. And, yes, I feel at home here,' Gabby explains. 'No one around for miles. There's something very grounding about being far away from the rest of civilisation.' She smiles. 'And this place has underfloor heating. Integrated lighting that mimics natural light so I can sleep well.'

'I hope you've got an alarm,' Anna says. 'CCTV.'

'There is an alarm, which I only use when I'm not staying here. No need for CCTV. No one ever drives up here and you can't even see the house from the road. Unless you know about this house, no one is coming all the way out here. No one's going to disturb us over the next few days.'

'Hmm,' Anna says. 'Still think I prefer the beach. I've spent many a night in the open air. You should all try it – there's nothing like staring up at the stars and realising how small and insignificant we are in this universe. Nature's more important than any of this.' She holds out her palms. 'No offence to anyone who loves, well, all this material stuff.'

I wonder if Gabby's offended by Anna's comments. She and Anna often clashed, which used to result in countless arguments. Many times I had to be the peacemaker.

'What are *you* doing with yourself these days, Shaun?' Anna asks, changing the subject.

'Shaun started his own tech company,' Gabby says, before he can answer for himself. 'Done really well for himself.' Her eyes are blank as she says this, her words coming out with no feeling accompanying them.

Anna smiles. 'Yeah, I noticed that beast of a car outside. Not concerned about the environment, then?' She doesn't wait for a response. 'And you, Finny?'

I'd forgotten how much Anna's intimate name for Fin used to bother me. Fin was never mine, though, although we teetered on the edge of becoming something. And I'm convinced we would have if neither of us had gone to Gabby's party that Christmas Eve. We nearly didn't. Fin's parents were out for the night and wouldn't be back until quite late, so he'd begged me to go to his place instead of the party. 'We can play truant,' he'd said, taking my hand, even though we'd never kissed. I'd known for a long time that Fin was interested in me as more than a friend, but it had only been in the lead-up to the party that I'd started to feel the same about him. My feelings had taken me by surprise – even though we'd always been close. So the unspoken promise of what would happen between us had tempted me to forgo the party, but in the end I'd put Gabby first. 'No, we all have to be there,' I'd said.

'I guess,' Fin had replied. 'We wouldn't want to get told off by our teacher, now, would we!' We'd laughed, but there was truth in his words. Sometimes, up until that night, it had felt as though Gabby was controlling us all.

Which is exactly how it feels now. Are we all puppets, summoned here by Gabby for some reason I can't bring myself to consider?

'I'm an aerospace engineer,' Fin tells Anna, in response to her question.

'I knew that obsession with science would get you somewhere,' Anna declares, raising her glass. 'Good for you, Finny.'

'Ha, I'll remind myself of that when I'm working my seven-day weeks,' Fin says.

'So, anyone have kids?' Anna asks, glancing at each of us in turn.

'Shaun has two,' Gabby says, once again speaking for him. I wonder how he feels about this – as far as I know, the two of them haven't seen each other for years, yet Gabby is being so overfamiliar.

Anna raises her eyebrows. 'Of all the people – I never thought Shaun would be the first to be a daddy. Who's the lucky mama?'

'My wife's called Alia. Married five years. Now, is it someone else's turn for a grilling?'

Anna glances at Gabby. 'This gets more intriguing by the minute.' She turns back to Shaun. 'And doesn't your wife mind you being away for Christmas?'

'She understands,' Shaun mumbles, a hint of red flushing his cheeks.

Raising her eyebrows, Anna turns her attention to Andre. 'And how about you, sweetie? What have you been up to all these years?'

Andre clears his throat. 'It's not what I'd planned to do, but I'm a chef. Not married yet.'

'Not just any chef,' Shaun says, slapping him on the back. 'Andre here is the head chef at the Ritz.'

'How about that,' Anna says. 'And Sasha is a teacher. What a noble cause. I couldn't do it. Well, look at us all. Look how far we've come.' Her voice fades, and she picks up her glass and downs what's left of her wine. I wonder how she knows what I do, when I haven't mentioned it in her presence.

'Your turn, Anna,' Shaun says. 'What is it you do?'

Anna shrugs. 'Oh, you know me. I don't like to be tied down to anything. People. Jobs. I work when I have to and the rest of the time I'm just... living. Anyway,' she says, turning to Gabby. 'What's this reunion about, Gabby?'

'Let's just enjoy each other's company,' Gabby says. 'No need to overanalyse everything, is there. I know you've come here for me, but isn't it good that we're all together again? Like this was always meant to happen. And now we have the next three days to get to know each other again. Who knows where it will take us?'

And when Gabby's eyes fix on me, a heavy lump wedges in my throat.

22:18

The guest room Gabby has put me in has a balcony overlooking the loch. Although it's freezing, and snow has already cast a white blanket across the ground, I throw my dressing gown over my pyjamas and stand outside, watching the shimmering water.

When someone knocks on the door, I expect it to be Gabby, making sure we're all settled for the night, but instead it's Fin standing there.

'Can I come in?' he asks.

'Um, yeah.' I let him in and watch as he sits on the chair by the bed. 'I'm feeling really uneasy about all this,' he says. 'I've been checking the weather, and the storm that's due to hit is major. Gabby must have known this.'

I've checked too, and Fin is right. Being stuck here in the middle of nowhere with no way to get home fills me with dread.

'And Anna,' Fin continues. 'She's still too much, isn't she? Asking us all that personal stuff straight away.'

'Anna's never had a filter,' I say.

'Remember when we thought it was refreshing that she spoke her mind? Now it just makes me uneasy,' Fin says.

But Anna's not the one I'm worried about.

'I noticed you kept quiet when Anna was asking everyone about their personal lives,' Fin says. 'Tell me to mind my own business, but is there anyone in your life?'

'Yes,' I say, noting the flash of disappointment on Fin's face. 'My dog, Scratch. We're inseparable.' I smile.

He smiles too. 'I loved you.'

Fin's comment comes out of nowhere and renders me speechless.

'We never had the chance to be together properly,' he continues. 'And it's always haunted me. And seeing you here tonight, I—'

'You're with someone,' I say.

'But seeing you makes me so confused.'

'It's because of what happened,' I say. 'That's the only reason.' It's an unbreakable tie that silently binds us. Fin must realise this too. 'Our feelings got mixed up in it.'

'Then surely that should make me want to run. Not the opposite.' Fin shakes his head. 'I only came here to see you. I said no at first, even though I felt bad for Gabby. And I would never have come, until she told me you were definitely coming.'

And that's exactly what she said to me about Fin. So she was lying to one of us. Or both. 'I think you should go,' I say. 'This is already complicated enough.' Terrifying is more the word, I think. 'Please, Fin.'

He does as I ask, turning back when he opens the door. 'I meant what I said.'

01:53

Something rouses me from an already fitful sleep and I peer through the blinds at the floodlit patio, shocked to see the heavy cascade of snow Gabby had warned us about already falling. I can't be trapped here. At the first sign of daylight, I will make my excuses and leave, before it gets any worse.

My throat feels dry; I forgot to bring a glass of water up with me when I came to bed, despite this being a habit at home. Using the torch on my phone to navigate my way downstairs, I stop at the bottom when I hear voices. They're coming from the living room, and the door is only slightly ajar – where this evening it was open – a dim shaft of light casting an orange glow onto the tiled floor.

I recognise Gabby's voice straight away, but it takes me a moment to register that it's Shaun she's talking to. Intrigued, I move closer to the door and listen. It feels wrong to stand here eavesdropping on what could be a private conversation, given their history, but I'm frozen. Gabby might reveal something about why she's asked us all to be here; if there's anyone she might confide in, it's Shaun. After all, the two of them were in a relationship, so she may still feel some sort of bond with him.

But their whispers are so low that even standing right by the door, I can't make out what they're saying. So instead, I peek through the door, ignoring the rush of guilt. And I'm once again frozen when I see what they're doing.

Gabby is naked, sitting on top of Shaun with her back to me. My hand clamps over my mouth to stifle my gasp. This is the last thing I expected to witness. Their relationship was over after that Christmas, yet now all it's taken is a few hours together to rekindle that flame. What is Gabby doing? Shaun is married with children.

I want to leave, to forget what I've seen, but I can't move, can't tear my eyes from them. When Shaun's hands reach up to Gabby's breasts, and she throws her head back and groans, I finally turn away.

And right behind me Andre stands, watching me.

THREE

NOW

Christmas Eve, 07:04

I barely sleep after seeing Gabby and Shaun together, and the look Andre gave me when he realised what I was doing has cemented itself in my head. Disgust. Disapproval. And something else I can't articulate. Something that made me feel uneasy.

I didn't wait to hear what he might say; instead, I rushed to my room. If he's got something to say about it he can message me, like he's been doing all these years. Never letting me forget.

It's still dark, and the house is silent when I get up and go downstairs to the kitchen. There are too many buttons on the expensive coffee machine, and for several minutes I fumble around, pressing every button until finally my cup begins to fill.

I take my coffee to the living room and sit on one of the accent chairs by the window. It's still snowing, and there must already be a foot of snow covering the ground. I need it to stop so I can leave.

There's a chill in the room, and I wonder how to turn the underfloor heating on. Probably with an app on Gabby's phone.

I pull the dressing gown I've borrowed from her tighter around me and cradle my mug.

Andre walks in when I'm staring out of the window, unable to see the loch as it's not yet sunrise. 'You're up early.' He's holding his own mug. 'From what I can tell it looks bleak out there,' he says. 'I can't see how we'll be able to leave after Boxing Day if this continues.' He studies my face. 'You look tired.'

My cheeks burn as I remember last night, and I pray he doesn't mention it. 'I think I'll leave today before it gets any worse. I can't get trapped here.'

Andre frowns and sits on the chair opposite mine. 'You can't leave. The party is tonight. Gabby's had this planned for months.'

'Doesn't that worry you?' I hiss. 'Doesn't this all feel weird?'

'I've got nothing to hide,' he says. 'I haven't done anything. My conscience is clear.'

He's having a dig at me, I know it. 'Why do you keep sending me those messages? What do you want from me, Andre?'

He sips his coffee and stares out of the window. 'What messages?'

'Does anyone know you've been contacting me all these years? Because Gabby seems to think this is the first time any of us has spoken to or seen each other since—'

'Sasha, I really don't know what you're talking about. Are you okay? I'm worried about you. And of all of us, I would have thought *you*'d be the one to stay away.'

I ignore his comment and turn away from his scrutiny, facing the loch again, marvelling at how nature can be at once sinister and calming. 'Why did you come here, Andre?'

'Same as you. For Gabby. Because it was our fault, wasn't it? We were the ones in the house. And it happened right under our noses. Of course I had to come when Gabby asked. For old times' sake, too. And because I've thought about all of you over the years. It feels like there's... unfinished business. Something like that. We know why Shaun's here,' he says. 'Clearly his marriage is a mess and he's fulfilling some fantasy by sleeping with Gabby again. But I'm surprised at you, watching them last night.'

'I wasn't. I just came downstairs to get some water. I didn't know they'd be... doing that. I thought things were over between them.'

'Is that what you were hoping? If I didn't know better, I'd think you had a thing for Shaun.'

I ignore his comment. 'Have you sent messages to the others?'

'What?'

'Is it just me you message?' I'm sure it is, but still I have to ask.

'Honestly, Sasha, I don't know—'

'And what are you two whispering about?'

We both look up to see Fin walking towards us.

'Nothing,' Andre says, picking up his cup and standing. 'I was just telling Sasha that it looks like we could all be snowed in soon. I've been reading the reports. When I can get reception, that is. Not looking good. Luckily, I don't have to rush back for anything.' He smiles. 'Sasha was telling me she's planning to leave today. Thankfully Gabby's got plenty of food in.'

Fin frowns and glances out of the window. 'Doesn't look good, does it?'

'Anyway,' Andre says. 'A nice hot shower's calling me.' He pats Fin on the back. 'Catch you later.' He turns to me. 'See you in a bit, Sasha.'

Fin eases into Andre's seat and leans forward, frowning. 'Are you okay? What was all that about you leaving today?'

'I can't be stuck here if the snow gets too deep to leave. I've got Scratch to think of. He's with my neighbour, but he'll miss me. He hates it when I go anywhere.'

'But you can't leave. One, it's not safe. And two, I really think Gabby knows something.' Fin reaches for my hand. Comforting and familiar, even after all this time. 'And that makes me worried for you.'

I, too, have wondered if Gabby knows I lied, but it doesn't make sense. 'Gabby would have come straight out and said it. Called the police. Why would she invite us all here pretending that she needs this for closure?'

'I don't know what she's doing, but think about it. She hasn't contacted a single one of us in twelve years. Why now? Something must have changed.'

'Maybe she's going to ask us again if we can remember anything.' Even I'm not convinced by my own words. 'But I can't, Fin. There's nothing but a huge blank.'

'Has nothing ever come back to you over the years?' Fin asks. 'Did you ever try to... I don't know... get help to try and recover those memories?'

I don't tell Fin that I've never wanted to remember. That it terrifies me more than anything. 'No. I've never remembered or got help. I was so out of it that night, Fin, though I don't remember drinking that much. Most of the night is a hazy blur.' Apart from being alone with Fin, the two of us about to change the direction of our friendship. And flashes of Seffie.

Even the aftermath only makes sense to me through the lenses of everyone else. I pull my hand away as I recall Andre's face when he saw me transfixed by what Gabby and Shaun were doing.

'I have to get in the shower,' I tell Fin.

He nods. 'But promise me you won't leave, will you? I can't bear the thought of you trying to drive anywhere in this.'

I leave without answering, because if anyone can convince me to stay, it's Fin.

14:20

The morning passes in a mixture of hushed conversations and anticipation. None of the others seem as anxious as me, and that only makes me more worried. They fear nothing. To them, I am the only one who has anything to lose by being here. Earlier, when I'd told Gabby I had to leave, she pointed out that my car would never make it through the snow. 'Shaun's might, at a push,' she'd said. 'And possibly Fin's. Until the snow gets too deep. But they're not crazy enough to attempt going anywhere so it looks like you're stuck here.' She'd smiled. 'You're safer here in this house.'

After a lunch of devilled eggs and honey-glazed ham, which everyone other than me has eaten with relish, we sit by the tree, as Michael Bublé belts out Christmas classics from hidden speakers.

'I do love Secret Santa,' Gabby announces, topping up our glasses with champagne. 'Drink up, everyone.' As she pours mine – a drink I won't touch – it's hard not to picture her and Shaun last night, the faint orange glow on their naked bodies. His hands roaming all over her. Their heavy breathing as they drank each other in. 'I think it's the anticipation of what we'll get,' Gabby continues. 'And who it could be from. I love the idea that we'll never know.' She rubs her hands together and reaches for the first present. 'Let's get this started.' She studies the tag, and hands it to Andre. 'For you, darling,' she says, kissing his cheek.

No one comments on it, but I notice his face flushing. 'Well, thanks, whoever this is from.' He peels off the wrapping paper slowly, as if he's trying to keep it intact, his eyebrows rising as he pulls out a bottle of whisky. 'This is... wow, what can I say? Thanks.' Behind his eyes, I see how he truly feels. Andre never drank spirits, and all of us knew it.

'No giving away who got it,' Gabby warns, smiling. She

takes the next present from under the tree. 'Shauny,' she says, giving him a kiss, this time a brief one on the mouth. Again, I recall the two of them last night. Shaun's muscular arms, the glow of his skin. A jolt courses through my body.

'Jeez, someone's pushed the boat out,' he says, holding up a bottle of Dom Pérignon. 'And as you all know – I'll drink anything.' He glances at Andre. 'Cheers, whoever you are.' He winks at Gabby.

'Don't look at *me*,' she says.

When it's Fin's turn, he flashes me a look filled with both anxiety and longing. He feels there's something looming, even if the others don't realise it. His present is the leather wallet I'd agonised over choosing, and I can tell, despite everything, he's pleased with the gesture. 'And just in time, as my old one is falling apart.'

'Ooh, I'm next,' Gabby says, ripping the gift wrapping like an excited child. 'This is beautiful,' she says, holding up a teal silk scarf.

With just me and Anna left, I begin to feel nervous. I tell myself it's just a silly Secret Santa game, but I can't shake the feeling that I should have left before we started, despite the relentless snow.

'Come on, Anna,' Gabby says, holding out the second-to-last gift – this one's for you.'

Anna smiles. 'Thanks, hun.' She takes the present and opens it, revealing a designer backpack that I see immediately is just her style. 'I love it!' she exclaims. 'I'm going to hug all of you as I'm not allowed to ask who it's from. I'll just have to pretend I know, though. So thoughtful.'

She seems genuinely touched as she makes her way around the coffee table, giving each of us a hug. When she reaches me, she whispers as she leans in for a hug, 'We need to find a moment to talk.'

'Right, last but not least,' Gabby declares. 'My darling

Sasha. This one's for you.' She holds it out to me and I wonder if she notices my hands are shaking as I take it. It's soft, and I wonder if it's also a silk scarf like Gabby's, although it feels too heavy.

'Maybe I'll open it later,' I say. 'Save it for tomorrow. I'm not used to opening presents early.'

'Nonsense,' Gabby says. 'It's Christmas Eve and we're finally all together after so very long. The celebration starts now.'

With all eyes on me, I take my time tearing the wrapping paper, as if I'm trying to preserve it to use again, and my body turns cold as I pull out my gift. I recognise it instantly, and my hand shakes. It's a silver skater-style dress, adorned in glimmering sequins. Beautiful. Made of expensive-feeling fabric.

'Th... thanks,' I say, forcing out the word.

'Oh, how lovely,' Gabby exclaims. 'You can wear it tonight!'

But it's a clear message to me, and I have no intention of wearing this dress. An identical version of the dress Gabby's little sister was wearing that Christmas Eve.

FOUR

NOW

14:34

With all eyes on me, I make an excuse that I need the bathroom, and rush from the room. The hum of chatter as I leave reassures me that no one is focusing on the Secret Santa gift I've received. But I can't be the only one who remembers that dress, can I?

In the bathroom, I lock the door and hold up the garment, studying it in the bright light. There's no brand label on it, no care instructions or size either, but I can tell it will fit me. It's identical to the one Seffie was wearing that night twelve years ago, only hers would have been child-sized. I remember how the sequins glinted in the light as she spun around, modelling it for us as we tried to encourage her to get to bed. *This is an adult party, Seraphina. Not for children.* Gabby's harsh words to her sister earlier that evening sound as if they're being spoken right now, in this bathroom in Scotland. The middle of nowhere.

Nausea churns in my stomach as I once again contemplate how no one noticed this dress is the same as Seffie's. I'm being sent a message – although I have no idea who gave it to me. But I know why I'm the one being targeted. Fin has been wondering if Gabby has another reason for bringing us all together, and she could have been the one to give me that gift, but without knowing this for sure, how can I trust any of them?

It takes me a few minutes to compose myself before I unlock the door and step back into the hall. Outside, the snow has given up its assault, even though I'm sure there's more on the way. I poke my head into the living room and announce that I'm going for a walk while the snow has let up.

'You can't go out there in this,' Gabby insists. 'It could start up again.'

'I need some fresh air. I'm used to walking my dog – I can't just stay inside. I won't be long.' I search Gabby's face – is she the one who got me that dress?

'I think it's crazy, but if you insist then you'll need wellies,' Gabby says. 'There's at least six inches of snow out there.'

She has a point. Of course I didn't bring wellies. It was all I could do to get myself here, so checking the weather was the last thing on my mind.

'I don't think it's safe,' Fin says, anxious frown lines appearing on his face. 'Just stay here with us,' he pleads. 'There could be more snow.'

'I'll be fine. I've got my phone. And I won't go far.'

'Just so you know, the reception around here is temperamental,' Gabby says. 'I can never rely on my phone.'

Her warning chills me, but I need to get out of here, if only for a few minutes. 'I need some fresh air,' I repeat.

'It's not fresh, it's freezing cold air,' Shaun says. 'You won't catch me going out there in this. Nope. I like my home comforts too much.' He stretches his arms behind his back and puts his feet up on the sofa.

'I can't sit still when I'm not working.' I'm explaining myself too much – making it too obvious that I'm unnerved.

Anna jumps up. 'I'll come with you. I've got hiking boots in my bag – they'll do. And we don't have to go far.'

I'm about to tell her I need to be alone, but I remember that earlier she'd said she wanted to talk to me. The only way I'll find out who gave me that dress, and who here is a threat to me, is if I spend more time with each of them. For years I've lived in shadows, giving up on my relationship with Jarred, on any relationship that could have bloomed, because of what happened, so now that I'm here, it's time I put an end to it.

'I'll just run upstairs and get my boots,' Anna says, tying her long dark hair into a ponytail. 'Don't leave without me.'

While she's gone, I take the dress to my room and spread it out on the bed. What I want to do is scrunch it up and shove it in the bin. Out of sight. But even disposed of, it will never be off my mind. And I won't stop seeing Seffie, twirling around, with lipstick she should never have been wearing.

Downstairs, Anna still hasn't appeared, so I pull on my heavy parka and search for Gabby's boots in the shoe cabinet by the door. There are rows of neatly arranged shoes, trainers and boots. All of which seem to belong to Gabby. There isn't a trace left here of her husband. I pull out the boots – Le Chameau, of course.

'Nice,' Anna says, appearing at the bottom of the stairs. She rolls her eyes. 'No expense spared on those, I'm sure. Are you ready?'

She's wearing a long padded coat that almost trails on the floor, and surely must belong to Gabby, who is easily three inches taller than Anna. 'At least it will keep me warm,' she says, patting the coat.

Outside, even though there's only a scattering of snow drifting from the sky, a fierce wind howls around us.

'Jesus,' Anna says, doing up her coat. 'I'm not used to this any more. Bit of a shock to the system. I've not seen less than twenty degrees for years.'

'Don't you ever come back?' I ask.

'Nope.'

'What about your parents? And your brother?'

'They're happy to visit me in Spain. I never come here.'

Yet she's here now.

Outside, solid snow crunches beneath our feet as we head away from the house, and it's clear that we won't be able to go far. Beyond the loch, the landscape of rugged mountains that should look serene and picturesque is now an ominous reminder that we are fast becoming trapped in this place. And the clouds taunt us with their threat of more snow.

'How can she live here?' Anna says, her thoughts clearly mirroring my own.

I stop and grab Anna's arm. 'Do you think Gabby asked us here just to help her move on?'

Anna frowns. 'What else would it be?'

'I'm not sure, but I can't help wondering if she's playing games with us.'

'Games? What does that mean?' Anna asks.

'She must have known about the snowstorm,' I say. 'It's all over the news. And have you seen how much food she's got in? If she didn't anticipate us being stuck here, why get so much food?'

'Because Gabby always plans ahead. You're reading too much into things, Sasha. Look, none of us really want to be here, do we? But we owe it to Gabby to help her.' Anna's eyes narrow. 'Some more than others.'

'And what's that supposed to mean?'

Anna turns away and continues walking, her hiking boots squelching in the snow. 'Let's not even go there,' she says. 'What we need to do is just be normal. Try to enjoy this Christmas.'

I stare at her, incredulous. 'You mean, pretend nothing happened.'

'If that's what Gabby needs us to do, then, yeah. What do you want us to do? Chat about it over hors d'oeuvres?'

'So you don't think there's another reason Gabby wanted us all here? After all this time?'

Anna stops walking. 'Sounds to me like a guilty conscience. You've got to let this go. The past is best left in the past, don't you think? Why bring it all up now? It's done. We can't rewrite anything.'

I stare at her; these words seem alien coming from the woman I knew her to be. Anna used to fight for things. People. Causes. She cared. 'I think you just need to keep moving forward,' she says. 'Don't look back. It doesn't do any good.' Perhaps I'm getting paranoid, but her words seem to be some kind of warning.

'We used to be close, didn't we?' I say. 'You and I had a connection.'

Anna nods, but looks away again. Avoiding eye contact is another thing she never used to do. 'Things change,' she says. 'We don't know each other any more. None of us know the first thing about each other.'

'Gabby and Shaun definitely do.' The words leave my mouth with no forethought. But it's too late to take them back.

Anna frowns. 'What does that mean?'

I have no choice now, so I tell her what I saw last night, and a flash of their naked bodies plants itself in my mind. The sense of something familiar.

'No way,' Anna says. 'That was over long ago. Why would they...' She trails off. 'You'd think people would learn a lesson about excessive drinking, wouldn't you?'

'I don't think anyone had too much last night,' I say.

'Speaking of lost love – what's up with you and Fin?' she asks. But there's no mischievous smile on her face, as there would have been years ago. Anna and I had spent many nights staying up until three a.m. discussing how much Fin liked me. She was his biggest supporter, urging me to give it a chance, in some ways even more than Gabby, who'd grown tired of hearing about why we hadn't got together.

'I don't get it,' she'd say. 'You're always together. What's stopping you?'

I knew exactly what was stopping me. Fear of losing him if it didn't work out. I never wanted to be his ex-girlfriend, so it felt safer to carry on being his friend. Until I realised that I wanted to take that chance after all.

'Fin's in a relationship,' I say to Anna. 'And I've just come out of one, so there's no way—'

'There was always some excuse, wasn't there? But this is *Fin* we're talking about. Sasha and Fin.' Anna smiles. 'I always thought I'd be coming to your wedding one day. Not that I believe in that meaningless piece of paper. It's just something to keep us prisoners. But… well, you believed in it, so it's something I always imagined for you.'

'Was that dress from you?' I ask, ignoring what Anna's just said. It's too painful to think of how I lost Fin that night, as well as everything else.

'What dress?'

'My Secret Santa gift. The silver sequinned dress.'

'No. It's nice, though. Not sure it would have been my choice, but you could totally pull it off.'

'Don't you see?' I ask, pulling her arm to stop her striding away.

'See what?'

'That dress is exactly the same as the one Seffie was wearing that night. Remember?'

Anna stares at me, and her face creases. She opens her mouth, then closes it again. Another thing I've never seen before: Anna is lost for words.

Eventually, she speaks. 'I don't know what you mean,' she says. 'Seffie definitely wasn't wearing a dress like that. You must be mistaken.'

FIVE

BEFORE

Christmas Eve, 2012

Sasha's body buzzes with excitement as she sits in Gabby's living room, staring at the brightly coloured tinsel and baubles hanging on the tree. Gabby's mum has clearly let Seffie decorate it, and Sasha resists the urge to rearrange the cluster of baubles hanging too closely together.

She glances at her phone; the others will be here soon. She feels giddy, like a kid, eagerly anticipating something. For three years, she and Fin have danced around the idea of getting together. Flirting, feeling the closeness of friendship with the question of something more wrapped around them. But either she's been in a relationship or Fin has. And Sasha would never betray someone she's with, even if her feelings for Fin lie deeper than anything she's felt for any of the others she's been with.

'Wow, look at you,' Gabby says as she comes downstairs. She eyes Sasha's royal-blue skater-style dress. It skims her body, rather than being figure-hugging like Gabby's dress, and she's much more comfortable being able to actually move. 'Hot stuff!' Gabby says, chuckling. 'Finley's in for a treat.'

They both burst out laughing, so hard that Sasha's stomach aches. 'Hot stuff? Sounds like something my parents would say,' she says, between fits of hysterics.

Gabby frowns. 'Seffie let you in then? I told her not to answer the door to anyone, but that kid just doesn't listen. Drives my parents insane. What *is* that? It's like since the day she was born, she wanted to defy everyone. And ten years later, nothing's changed.'

'She'll be a force to reckon with when she's older,' Sasha says. 'I say good for Seffie.'

'Well, you're welcome to have her. You always said your mum wished she'd tried for another. Well, please take her.'

'What are you saying about me?' Seffie appears in the doorway; it wouldn't be surprising if she'd been standing there the whole time. As much as Sasha likes her, she has that unnerving way of creeping up on you, taking you by surprise. It's infuriating.

'Nothing!' Gabby barks. 'I thought I told you to stay in your room. This is an adult night. You're ten. That means scoot!'

'You know Mum and Dad would kill you if they knew you were having a party,' Seffie says, her hands on her hips. 'People might mess up the house.' So mature for a ten-year-old.

'Don't you worry about any of that, Seraphina,' Gabby says. 'These are my friends, not just anyone. They'll take great care. Now please, can you just stay in your room, okay?'

Seffie rolls her eyes and walks out. 'Glad to see you've got some Christmas spirit, sister,' she shouts. 'Can't wait to see what happens when Mum and Dad find out.'

'They won't though, will they?' Gabby shouts to her sister's disappearing back. 'So you'd better keep your mouth zipped.'

Gabby's threat hovers in the room. Lately, Sasha's been questioning just how good a friend she is, and analysing all her actions. If someone can treat their sister so contemptuously, then what does that say about their character? Still, they've been through a lot together since they met that first day at university. The others came a little later, but Gabby was there right from the start, in Sasha's first literature lecture, and they clicked from the moment they opened their mouths to speak.

Sasha checks her phone again, smiling when a message from Fin appears.

'Will you please do us all a favour and just sleep with him already?' Gabby says, laughing. It's clear she's already been drinking. Over the last few months, there's rarely been a night for her that didn't involve alcohol.

'This is not like you and Shaun,' Sasha says. 'Fin and I aren't love's young dream. We haven't even kissed. There might be no chemistry.'

'Oh, nonsense. You've got more chemistry than a science lab! I don't understand what the problem is. He clearly adores you, and I see how you look at him.'

Sasha's cheeks flush. 'Yeah, well. Let's see what happens.'

'Oh, yes. Tonight is a blank page waiting to be written on.' Gabby laughs. 'And it will be... an erotic tale!'

Sasha shakes her head. 'Very funny. Ever thought of doing stand-up?'

Gabby disappears and comes back holding an unopened bottle of Prosecco. 'Courtesy of the parents,' she says. 'They're not big drinkers so I doubt they'll even notice.'

She pours two glasses and they sink into Gabby's large corner sofa.

'Actually, Sash, there's something I wanted to talk—' The doorbell rings. 'Never mind. It can wait.'

Sasha hears Andre's voice and she gets up to greet him. He's quiet and reserved, but Sasha respects that about him. He prefers to listen rather than hear the sound of his own voice, and compared to someone like Shaun, it's a refreshing change.

'Hey, Sasha – you look nice,' he says.

She curtseys. 'Thanks. Thought I'd better make an effort as it's Christmas.'

Andre looks around the room at the brightly coloured tinsel and garlands hung in every available space, and the nativity scene displays, candy canes and stockings hung above the mantelpiece. 'Don't we just know it?'

'Yeah, I think Gabby's parents are the type to put up the tree in summer and not take it down until Easter. Shh, don't tell her I said that.'

Andre laughs, even though what Sasha's said isn't that funny. 'Fin not here yet, then?' he asks, sitting on the sofa.

'On his way with Shaun. How's your master's going? Is it weird being at uni without us?'

'Hmm. Actually, it's kind of peaceful,' Andre says, and Sasha gently punches his arm.

Gabby comes back in. 'Sorry, just had to sort Seffie out. Why do I get the feeling she's going to be a little pain in my arse tonight?'

'Give her a break,' Andre says. 'She's your little sis. You're responsible for her while your parents are away.'

Gabby flashes a smile. 'And aren't I the lucky one?'

When Fin arrives with Shaun, he takes Sasha's hand and spins her around. 'Well, look at you, Sash. You scrub up well.'

'Thanks. I'll take that as a compliment.' Sasha folds her arms around him, inhaling the scent of his aftershave. And when she pulls away, Andre is watching them.

'Where *is* Anna?' Gabby asks, tutting. 'She always has to be the last to arrive. I even told her seven thirty so she'd actually be here on time.'

Shaun walks up to her and nuzzles her neck, and although Gabby smiles, she pushes him away. 'I need another drink,' she says.

Sasha joins her in the kitchen and watches as she pulls

another bottle from the wine cooler. 'Do you think maybe you should slow down, Gabby? It's still quite early.'

'It's Christmas!' Gabby screeches, lifting the bottle. 'And we're celebrating.' She pours herself a glass. 'Happy Christmas!'

'Do you think Andre's okay?' I ask. 'He seems really quiet. I mean, more than usual.'

Gabby shrugs. 'Course he's not okay.'

'What do you mean?'

'Oh, nothing. Come on, drink up.' Gabby looks past Sasha to the door. 'Get out!' she screams.

Sasha spins around and Seffie is standing there, dressed in lilac pyjamas, once again appearing out of nowhere like an apparition. 'How am I supposed to sleep with all this noise?' she moans.

Gabby shrugs. 'It's Christmas songs! You love them. Just go to bed,' she snaps.

Seffie looks taken aback, and when she stalks off, Sasha feels sorry for her. All she wants to do is be a part of her older sister's life. To fit in somehow, despite her young age. To have some attention from someone. Isn't that what everyone wants?

'You shouldn't be so hard on her,' she says to Gabby once Seffie's left. But her friend's not listening. She's staring at her reflection in the kitchen French doors, rearranging the black bodycon dress she's wearing. For Shaun's benefit, Sasha's sure.

Sasha leaves her to it and heads upstairs to find Seffie. Just to make sure she's okay. At the top of the stairs, she hears voices, and there is Seffie talking to Andre, giggling at something he's just said. When he sees Sasha, he rushes over. 'Hey, I was just telling Seraphina that she should probably be in bed.'

'Okay, okay, I'm going,' Seffie says, slamming the door shut.

'Let's go down,' Andre says, glancing at the closed door.

'Why were you up here anyway?' Sasha asks.

'Just using the bathroom.'

But there's one downstairs, and when Sasha walked past it just now there was nobody in it.

SIX

NOW

16:19

I need to talk to Fin, yet every time I've tried since I got back from my walk with Anna, there's someone else demanding his attention. I need one of the others to confirm that they, too, remember Seffie wearing a dress like the one I was given, that I'm not going mad.

In the kitchen, I help Gabby and Anna prepare the buffet food for this evening. Sausages wrapped in bacon, shrimp cocktails, stuffed mushrooms, and other things I don't even know the names of. There's so much of it, more than just the six of us could ever get through, but I keep quiet. Gabby has always been intent on doing things her way.

'Are you sure you're okay?' Anna asks Gabby. 'I mean, it can't be easy celebrating like this on Christmas Eve.' I'm surprised Anna is mentioning this, after earlier insisting we should forget the past.

Gabby stops placing stuffed mushrooms on a tray. 'For twelve years I haven't celebrated. What's there to celebrate? Christmases have passed and I've always had my head buried in a glass. But I'm not doing that any more. Tonight, everything changes. I can't change what happened, but I can make sure I find a way to live with it. Properly, I mean. Not just going through the motions.'

'Is that why we're here?' Anna asks, glancing at me.

'I think it's just time to lay things to rest, isn't it?' Gabby flashes me a smile and I force myself to match her gesture, but my mouth feels as though it will crack.

'Well, that all sounds very healthy,' Anna says, giving Gabby a hug. 'Here if you need me, lovely.'

'I know,' Gabby says, twisting pastry into cheese straws.

My chance to talk to Fin comes an hour later, when everyone's getting ready for the evening. I knock on his door, hoping to catch him alone.

'Sash,' he says, 'come in. I'm glad it's you. Shaun's been bugging me about investing in his company. I made the mistake of telling him I've managed to save up quite a bit and I'm looking for something to invest in. Not sure it's a good idea to mix friendship with business.'

'I'm no expert, but probably not,' I say, shutting the door.

'What's up, Sash? You don't seem... I mean, I know I haven't seen you for years, but I can still tell when something's wrong. Well, I know being here in the first place is what's wrong, but has something happened?'

'That dress,' I begin. 'The one someone gave me for my Secret Santa gift – didn't you recognise it?'

Fin frowns. 'I don't know. Maybe. Why?'

'It's identical to the one Seffie was wearing that night.'

Fin scrunches his face, taking his time to answer. 'Are you sure? I thought she was wearing pyjamas? Weren't they purple? Or blue? Something like that.'

'Yes, she was wearing lilac pyjamas. But don't you remember that she changed at some point during the evening? I have no idea why, but she came downstairs in a party dress identical to the one I was given. I think it was when Gabby had gone. I don't think she would have dared come down with it on while Gabby was still there. Do you remember, she kept shouting at Seffie. She was horrible to her.'

'And I'm sure she hates herself for that now. Jesus. If we could live that day again. I wouldn't even go to that stupid party. I didn't want to, remember? We should never have gone. Our lives would be so different now.'

'But we did go, Fin.'

'Do you remember when we were alone?' Fin asks. 'When we were on the sofa in the garden office. We kept the light off so it was dark and it felt like there was no one else around. Even though we could hear those Christmas songs playing in the house.'

This memory is hazy for me, but it's still just about there, fuzzy around the edges. Incomplete.

'I told you that I loved you,' Fin continues. 'And we were going to... you know. But then you needed some water. You had that weird headache. And we were never alone again after that.'

I need to change the subject. 'All these years, haven't you wondered what happened to Seffie?'

Fin looks away. 'All the time. But it doesn't do any good to wonder. We just don't *know*.'

'I wish I could remember something. Anything. It scares me to think that—'

Fin takes my hand. 'I think maybe you're better off not remembering.'

'But what if it was one of us,' I say. 'We were the only ones in that house.'

'Someone could have come in and—'

'The police never found any evidence to support that theory. Did they? All they found was a trace of blood in her room that could have been there for days.'

Fin sits down on the bed. 'Have you ever thought it was me?'

'I've thought it was each one of you at different times. Of course I have. But I don't believe it was you. You were nowhere near Seffie.'

I join him on the bed, and when my leg touches his, a jolt of electricity shoots through my body, stronger than I remember it being before. How is it still possible that being close to Fin can do this to me? After all this time, and after the events of that night? 'We all have a reason for coming here,' I say. 'You said yours was to see me again. Mine is to face what happened, because I knew this day would come. But it feels like one of us is here to make someone pay. And being given that dress makes me think I'm the someone.'

Fin wraps his arms around me. 'It could just be coincidence. It's so easy to read too much into things.'

'Gabby's been off with me,' I say. 'And even on the phone inviting me here she was... I don't know – distant. We used to be close. What if she doesn't believe I can't remember anything? When she ignored my messages after it happened, that cemented in my mind that she thinks I'm the guilty one.'

'Gabby's often off with people,' Fin says. 'That doesn't mean she thinks you did something.'

Fin always liked to think the best of people. It was one of the things that drew me to him. His belief that people are inherently good. How did what happened to Seffie not change that? I want to believe that I'm wrong, and this is just Gabby's way of moving on. But my Secret Santa gift says otherwise.

'You were worried earlier,' I say. 'About why we're all here. Aren't you any more?'

Fin lets out a deep breath. 'Yes. But being with you makes me not care. You mean more to me than anything Gabby could say.'

I smile, and kiss his soft lips.

'Look,' he says. 'I... I didn't mention it before, and wasn't going to tell anyone... but Ravinder and I are separating. It hasn't been working for a long time. She moved out a few days ago.'

Acting on impulse, I reach for him and pull him closer, my mouth searching for his. The taste of him is exactly how I always imagined it would be, and my whole body stirs. His hands search every part of me, tugging at my clothes, and I do the same to him, desperate to feel his skin against mine.

'I want you so much,' he breathes into my ear, as I feel how hard he is against my body. This is a bad idea, my brain insists, but my body shuts the thought away, and I push Fin backward onto the bed and climb on top of him, not even bothering to fully undress.

Afterwards, Fin grips me tightly, as if I'll disappear if he lets go. 'Are you okay?' he asks, still breathless.

I nod, and for a few seconds I feel elated, until the reality of all of us being here smothers it.

Fin strokes my cheek. 'You have to stop worrying,' he says. 'If Gabby thought you'd done something, she would have said something. Everything will be okay. I don't know what she's doing, but I honestly don't think it's just about you.'

'But the dress,' I say.

'Coincidence.' Fin kisses my cheek. 'I'm sure of it.'

His phone vibrates on the bedside table and a name flashes on the screen, just long enough for me to catch it before the screen fades to black.

Ravinder.

Without realising I've seen it, he continues talking. Telling me how we need to just get through these next couple of days, and then we'll all be out of here.

'I need to go,' I say, grabbing my bra and pulling on my

jumper. I feel exposed and vulnerable, despite what just happened with Fin. How good it felt. 'I have to get ready,' I explain, to prevent him questioning me.

He pulls me back and kisses me. 'You don't regret this, do you?'

I shake my head, but the truth is I don't know. I vowed to stay away from all five of them, and this feels like playing with fire.

SEVEN

NOW

19:30

I hold up the silver dress and take a deep breath before slipping it over my head. It fits perfectly, and it chills me to think that whoever bought it knew what size to get.

But I will wear it. To prove that I'm not unnerved by any of this, just as none of the others seem to be. If we're all going to be trapped in this house together, then I will make sure I find out the truth. Coming here has to be for something.

There is music playing when I get downstairs – a mixture of Christmas classics and current music, just like Gabby had played that night. I've barely been able to listen to Christmas songs since then, avoiding radio stations just before December, and it surprises me that Gabby wants to hear them. It's as if she is recreating that Christmas Eve – but why? This time, though, no one is dancing. Gabby and Shaun are engrossed in conversation near the fireplace, and Fin and Anna are debating something on the other side of the room. Doesn't he remember that it's impossible to win an argument with Anna?

Andre sits in a chair by the windows, tapping something

into his phone. I'm about to go over to him and thank him for the dress, to see what reaction it garners, but Anna beats me to it, abandoning her debate with Fin and sliding onto the arm of Andre's chair. He looks up and shifts over as she leans in to speak to him.

'I know you're worried about that dress,' Fin says, appearing beside me, 'but you do look amazing in it.' He stares at me with hungry eyes, taking in every inch of me. 'But even better with it off,' he whispers, his lips brushing my ear.

Ignoring the frisson of excitement I feel, that physical need for him that hasn't been sated even though we just slept together, I tell him I'm going to find out what happened to Seffie. *Even if all roads lead to me.*

He frowns. 'Maybe you should let it go,' he says. 'This isn't healthy. We'll never know—'

I don't listen to the rest, but walk towards Gabby, who's throwing her head back and laughing at something Shaun has just whispered in her ear.

'Hey. Everything okay?' I ask. Because despite how hard she's pretending otherwise, tonight can't be easy for her.

'Everything's great!' she slurs. 'Absolutely perfect.'

I gesture to her glass. 'Gabby, how much have you had?'

'Really, Sasha? This isn't like twelve years ago. I actually stopped drinking. But now... maybe I just don't care any more.' She raises her glass. 'Cheers to that!' She takes in my dress. 'By the way, that looks wonderful on you. It's as if it was made for you.' She turns back to Shaun, letting me know that this conversation is over.

Shaun shrugs. 'She's fine. We need to all just relax and try to enjoy ourselves. That's what Gabby needs.' He strokes her cheek. 'Right?'

'And how's your wife doing?' I ask.

Fin nudges me, but I ignore his warning.

'And what's that supposed to mean?' Shaun says.

I shake my head and walk away.

'What was that all about?' Fin asks, when he catches up with me.

'Nothing. It doesn't matter.'

Turning away, I notice that Andre and Anna are no longer sitting in the chair by the window. I scan the room but there's no sign of them.

'Where did they go?' I ask Fin, pointing to the empty chair.

He shrugs. 'Maybe to get some more drinks?'

'I need the bathroom,' I say, slipping away before Fin can question me further.

'Do They Know It's Christmas?' begins to play as I leave, taunting me. It's the last song I remember hearing that night, even though many more were played. The night stopped for me, but nobody else.

There's no sign of either Andre or Anna anywhere downstairs, and with the snow falling heavily enough to obscure the view of the loch, it's unlikely they've ventured outside. Gabby's warned us several times it's not safe out there, and that we'll all just need to sit it out. Did she know this would happen?

I make my way upstairs, the silver dress rustling against my skin, feeling heavy on my body. It's silent up here, with only the faint echo of the music filtering from downstairs. At night-time this house feels eerie and ominous, and I wonder how Gabby can stand to be here on her own, especially after Seffie. Especially with barely any security other than an alarm she never uses and a doorbell camera.

As I pass Gabby's bedroom, I hear a noise coming from inside, even though she's downstairs. Taking a deep breath, I push the door open, stunned to see Anna in there, crouched down, rummaging through Gabby's chest of drawers.

She's so engrossed in whatever she's doing that she doesn't notice I'm watching her.

'Anna? What's going on?'

Her head jolts up and she jumps to her feet, shoving the drawer closed. 'Nothing... I...'

Checking to make sure no one else is around, I close the door. 'Why are you going through Gabby's things?'

For the first time I can remember, Anna falters, taking her time to respond. 'Please don't tell Gabby.'

'I need to know what you were doing, Anna.'

Anna closes the drawer she had open and sits on the bed.

'You think Gabby's planned something, don't you?' I say. 'Is that what you're doing in here? Looking for evidence?'

Anna shakes her head. 'No... you've got it all wrong. You need to get over this, Sasha. Let it go. Look, I understand why you're worried. I would be, too, if I couldn't remember what happened that night. You must have all sorts of doubts in your head.'

'No,' I lie. 'I know I had nothing to do with it.'

Anna tilts her head, as if she pities me. 'Well, Gabby doesn't know anything. She would have come right out and said it. Or gone to the police. This is Gabby we're talking about. Always spoke her mind, didn't she?'

Is Anna right? Or has Gabby resorted to playing twisted games? 'But she must have known about the storm,' I say. 'It's all over social media and the local news here. Haven't you been checking your phone?'

'I can barely get any reception,' Anna says.

'Then what *are* you doing in here, Anna?'

She pulls me towards the bed and ushers me to sit. 'Will you promise you won't say a word to anyone? I can't have the others knowing. None of them.'

'Okay.' Yet how can I make this promise when I have no idea what she's about to say, or if it might impact us all?

'I have a problem,' Anna begins, scratching at her arm. 'Sometimes I... sometimes I steal things.' She looks down at the red mark she's just made on her skin.

I'm speechless. This is so far removed from anything I expected Anna to say. 'What?'

'I'm sure you've heard of it.' Anna sighs. 'Kleptomania. But I don't like to put labels on myself. I'm not going to let anyone else define who I am.'

'When did it start?' I ask, still struggling to process what she's telling me.

She looks at me with her dark, wide eyes, and beyond the ferocity I see a damaged woman. Just as I am. 'It was after Seffie, wasn't it?'

She shakes her head. 'No, it's got nothing to do with that. I was doing it before.'

I take her arm. 'This is serious, Anna. What... what kind of things do you steal?'

'Nothing huge. I don't even want the stuff I take. It's not valuable. It's just... I can't seem to help it.' She looks at me, her eyes searching to understand what I'm thinking. All I know is that even Anna is capable of shame.

'Did you take something that night? Something of Seffie's?' I need to know this.

She buries her head in her hands, a gesture that's so alien to the Anna I know. When she looks up, her eyes are hard and cold once again. 'Yes,' she says. 'Just that cheap bracelet she was always wearing. I'm sorry.'

'Anna!' I gasp. 'Why? You can't—'

'Oh, don't worry. I didn't know what was going to happen, did I? And then it was too late to put it back. Anyway, I threw it in the sea when I first got to Málaga. It seemed like the right thing to do. Kind of like part of her was in that vast ocean. Kind of free. It made me feel better to think of it like that.'

'What if you'd been caught with it?' I can't help raising my voice.

'Keep it down, will you? Look, all it would prove is that I steal things. Not a big deal, Sasha.'

But what Anna's just told me has sickened me. She took something of Seffie's. Held onto it for months.

'Don't shame me,' she says, when I can't bring myself to say anything. 'I'm not proud of stealing things. But like I said, they're not expensive.'

'Value isn't just about money,' I point out. 'That bracelet could have helped Gabby. Don't you think she deserves to have something that meant so much to her sister?'

Anna rolls her eyes. 'Thanks for the lesson, Miss Hunt. Like I said, I couldn't put it back after I'd taken it. It was much earlier in the evening I took it. It must have fallen off and I slipped it in my pocket.'

'I'm sorry. This is just a bit of a shock. It's taken me by surprise.'

Anna touches my dress. 'You've come to your senses then? Realised there's no sinister motive for us all being here?'

I study Anna's face. It's hard to believe she is the one who gave me this dress. She's too straight-talking for that. She would tell me to my face if she had something to say. 'I hope you're right,' I concede.

'Anyway, we'd better get back downstairs before someone misses us,' Anna says, standing and smoothing down her own dress. 'And before Gabby drinks herself into oblivion.'

'I'll be right down,' I say. 'Just desperate for the bathroom.'

She leaves me alone and I head to Gabby's en suite, stopping when I hear the bedroom door shut and I'm alone.

Now that I'm in Gabby's room, I take the opportunity to search it, just in case there is anything that might prove she's planned something. That she knows what we did.

The archway next to the en suite leads to a walk-in wardrobe and I step inside, amazed at the amount of clothes lining each wall, given that Gabby doesn't spend that much time here. All of them are in colour order from lights to darks. I recall how Gabby's clothes were always strewn across the floor when we shared a student flat, and wonder when she became so obsessively organised.

Pushing aside the guilt I feel at intruding into her life like this, I search behind her clothes, but there's nothing hidden anywhere. Then in the corner I spot a separate mirrored wardrobe. Opening it, I find myself staring at a shelving unit with a computer screen, and on it there are CCTV cameras showing every room in the house.

Even the bedrooms.

EIGHT

NOW

20:24

I stare at the screens, horrified. Gabby told us she didn't have CCTV, yet I'm staring at my friends in the living room, and the empty bedrooms. All except Gabby's are on the screen.

She could have been watching me with Fin earlier. I turn up the volume, but it doesn't appear that there's any sound. That does little to ease my fear, and with the snow falling so heavily outside, the chances of us being able to leave are dwindling.

Checking the door to the bedroom is still closed, I fumble around with the mouse attached to the screen, trying to work out how to switch the cameras off. It takes me a while, but eventually I manage to shut them all down. If Gabby notices, hopefully she'll think it's just a technical fault. And in her heavily inebriated state, this should buy me some time.

I consider going downstairs to confront her with her lie, but if Gabby doesn't know I'm aware of the cameras, I could use it to my advantage.

Back in my own bedroom, I pull the silver dress over my

head and throw it on the floor. Rummaging through my suitcase, I find the black dress I always planned to wear and slip it on. And with this change of clothes comes an intense sense of relief, despite discovering the hidden cameras. Whatever this is, it's far from over.

Downstairs, I hear raised voices in the kitchen. Gabby and Shaun.

'You need to get a grip, Gabby,' Shaun says.

'Really? Let go of me.'

'This isn't my fault. I don't know what the fuck happened to Seffie!'

'You were there. You were all there. One of you knows what happened to her.'

'The police questioned us all, and they let us go. They thought she must have been abducted or that she ran away.'

'That doesn't mean they got it right.' Gabby's words are so slurred I can barely make out what she's saying, even though she's shouting.

'Haven't you ever stopped to wonder if she wanted to disappear?' Shaun says. 'You were always so horrible to her.'

Seconds of silence tick by.

I expect Gabby to snap, but she remains calm. 'Seffie would never have run away,' she says. 'She was happy. And how do you explain that blood on her bedroom door!'

'That could have been from anything. And Seffie was going through some stuff at school, wasn't she?' Shaun says. 'You told me about it. She was struggling to keep friendships, and was always on her own. Maybe she'd had enough and—'

I hear the sound of flesh being slapped, and I can only assume Gabby has struck Shaun's face. She always did have a temper when she'd been drinking. 'The truth's going to come out tonight, Shaun, I promise you. Why do you think you're all here? Do you really think I just wanted to sleep with you again?

That I couldn't resist one more piece of you?' Gabby cackles. 'Ha, wrong, Shauny.'

'I think you should go and sleep this off,' Shaun says, surprisingly calm given what Gabby's just announced.

'Don't patronise me. I won't be silenced. By you or anyone else. I want the truth, whatever it costs me to get it.'

More silence follows before Shaun responds. 'What was last night about, then? Why did you sleep with me?'

When Gabby answers, her voice is measured, despite how much she's had to drink. 'We were supposed to, that Christmas Eve, weren't we? Before I went to help my neighbour? Before everything kicked off. You'd been trying to get me alone all night.'

'And if I remember, you were keeping your distance. Why? I never did find out.'

'What happened last night was the last time. You and I will never do that again,' Gabby says. 'Never. Do you understand?'

Gabby stalks out of the kitchen, not noticing that I'm hovering by the study door.

I follow her; she's in a terrible state and, despite everything she's just said, I need to check she's okay. 'Gabby, wait.'

But she ignores me. Clutching the banister, she stumbles upstairs, surprisingly fast for someone so intoxicated.

She reaches her room and tries to shut the door, but I thrust my arm out to stop it closing. 'I just want to make sure you're okay,' I say.

'Just go away, Sasha. Go back to the party. Leave me alone.'

Ignoring her, I step inside, shutting the door behind us. Gabby groans and sinks onto her bed, stretching her arms out behind her. I sit on the chair by the window. 'I'll just stay with you for a bit. Make sure you're okay.'

'Of course *I'm* okay,' she says, leaning up onto her elbows. 'You're the one who's not okay.'

'What does *that* mean?'

'Oh, Sasha. Haven't you worked it out by now?'

My chest tightens and I stare at her, desperate to know what she means but equally hoping her eyes will close and she'll fall asleep before she can say anything else. And this conversation will be long forgotten. I glance at her walk-in wardrobe, where the CCTV monitor hides.

'You need to get out of here,' she warns. And then she laughs. A cackling sound that chills my blood. 'Oh, I forgot – it's too late. You can't go anywhere. The six of us are stuck here now. And who knows when the roads will be clear again.'

I cross to her bed and sit beside her. 'We were good friends, weren't we? Before. Please, just tell me what we're all doing here. What's this all about, Gabby?' *But I won't mention the cameras.*

Gabby studies my face for a moment and then opens her mouth to speak, but instead flops back on the bed. 'Just leave me alone now, Sasha. I just want to be on my own.'

'Okay.' I stand. 'But I'll come back and check on you in a bit.'

Gabby waves me off. 'Just go. Fuck off, Sasha. And don't forget to enjoy yourself down there while you can.'

20:59

'Where's Gabby?' Anna asks, when I get back downstairs. 'Did she talk to you? We can't get her to say anything much. Nothing that makes sense, at least.'

I keep quiet about the warning Gabby gave me, that I need to get out of here. 'She's just having a rest. Does anyone know how to turn this music down? It's too loud.'

'I'll do it,' Shaun says, pressing something on a small panel on the wall. 'There. Better?'

'Yes. And now we're here without Gabby, we need to talk, don't we?' The cameras are off so we should be safe just talking.

Even if Gabby checks and realises they're switched off, it didn't seem as if there was any sound on them.

'What's this all about?' Shaun asks.

'You *know* what this is about,' I cry. 'Why are you all pretending nothing happened? One of us knows what happened to Seffie!'

'Keep your voice down!' Anna warns. 'Gabby might hear you. Seffie ran away. Or someone broke into the house and took her.'

'You don't really believe that,' I insist. 'And neither did the police at the time. Seffie didn't run away. And that means someone is lying.'

Fin takes my arm and urges me to sit. 'Please, just calm down, Sasha. We can talk this through rationally.'

I pull away. 'Stop!'

'We have to let this go,' Shaun says. 'I've spent years putting it behind me. I don't want to rake it all up now. This was supposed to be about us coming together for Gabby, so that she could move on, not dwell on what happened.'

I ignore his callous comment. 'We were the only ones in the house. And Gabby was at the neighbour's. We were supposed to be keeping an eye on Seffie. Keeping her safe.' My words feel like knives in my throat.

No one speaks, but they all glance at each other.

'You were the one Gabby asked to keep an eye on Seffie,' Anna says. 'I didn't even know Gabby had gone anywhere.'

I want to argue back, but Anna is right. That much is my fault. I should have checked on Seffie. Maybe I did. I wish I could force the memories to flood back.

'That's a bit harsh,' Fin says. 'Look, we just need to be here for Gabby. To support her with whatever she needs. And Seffie might still turn up one day. You often hear about missing people showing up years later.'

Seffie would be twenty-two now, almost the age Gabby was

at that party. And even though Seffie looked quite different to her sister, I picture her as an identical version of Gabby whenever I remember that she's older now. 'What she needs is closure,' I say.

Fin doesn't look at me, but turns to Anna.

'Don't you get it?' Anna says. 'Sasha, this is all about you. You were the last one to see Seffie that night. And you can't even remember anything.'

'I... I'd had too much to drink.'

'You hadn't, Sasha,' Shaun says. 'You'd only had a couple.'

I stare at him. 'What are you saying?'

'Sasha, surely you can see what's going on? We've all been protecting you.' He glances at Fin. 'We think you know what happened to Seffie and somehow you've just blocked it out.'

'No,' I say, as my whole body feels as if it's been set alight. 'No.'

I turn to Andre, but he looks away.

'Just for the record,' Fin says, 'that isn't what I think.'

'Oh, and why is that?' Shaun snorts. 'Rose-tinted glasses?'

Anna sighs. 'Am I going to have to say this?' She takes my hand. 'It's obvious that Gabby thinks you killed her sister.'

NINE

BEFORE

Sasha watches Gabby dancing in the middle of the room. She's throwing her head back and roaring with laughter, but she's the only one dancing so it's not clear what she's laughing at. Given the amount of Prosecco she's consumed, though, she doesn't need anything to set her off. The rest of them sit on the sofa, watching Gabby with a mixture of amusement and bewilderment.

Shaun nudges Sasha. 'Do you know what's going on with Gabby?' he asks.

'She's just a bit plastered. Better seeing her laughing than crying, though, right?' *And Gabby can be prone to either*, she thinks to herself.

'I don't mean that,' Shaun says. 'We're all a bit shitfaced, aren't we? I just mean... Gabby's been a bit... kind of distant, lately.'

Sasha chuckles. 'She's always all over you. If that's what you call keeping her distance, then—'

'Oh, yeah, she's fine when we're around you lot. But it's like she's putting on a show. When we're alone, she, um, hasn't let me anywhere near her for weeks. Barely even a hug.'

'Um, I don't think you should be telling me all this. Maybe it would be better to talk to Fin about it.'

'You're her closest friend,' Shaun says. 'I just thought she might have talked to you. You know, if there was something bothering her.'

There's a loose fragment of something in Sasha's mind, but she can't quite grasp it. Did Gabby say something to her? She doesn't think so. 'No, she hasn't said anything to me. She's just been really excited about this party. Gabby loves Christmas, doesn't she?'

'Okay,' Shaun says, but the frown remains on his face.

'Shaun, what's going on?'

'I just don't want her messing me around.'

Sasha jabs Shaun's arm. 'Gabby would never do that.' She points to his glass. 'I think you've had a bit too much of that. Gabby loves you, you fool.'

He nods. 'Yeah, course she does.' But his words don't sound convincing. 'I'm just being... anyway, your glass is empty.'

'Don't mind if I do,' Sasha says, handing him her glass. 'And everything's fine. Gabby loves you.'

When Shaun gets up to leave, Anna appears and slips into his seat. 'Hey,' she says. 'Is it me or are we all off our faces already? It's not even nine!'

'Speak for yourself. I am totally in control,' Sasha says. 'I've hardly had any. I'm pacing myself tonight.'

'Oh yeah? Any particular reason?' Anna laughs and nods towards Fin.

'We'll see. I haven't decided yet,' Sasha says. 'I just don't want to ruin our friendship.'

Anna raises her neat, thick eyebrows. 'Fuck friendship when you can have great sex! I know which one I'd choose.' She laughs. 'Anyway, what was Shaun talking about just now?'

'Not much. Himself.' Even though Sasha could trust Anna with what he said, she doesn't like to gossip. Anna might like

Shaun as a friend, but they all know she doesn't consider him suitable boyfriend material for Gabby, not when he'd worked his way through so many of the girls at their university before setting his sights on her. But Gabby had known all about his reputation. 'I'm on a mission to tame him,' she'd joked. And surprisingly, it seems to have worked.

Anna rolls her eyes. 'Typical, self-obsessed Shaun.'

When Shaun doesn't come back with Sasha's drink, she hunts for him in the kitchen. Gabby is alone in there, talking on her phone, blocking one ear so she can hear whoever's on the other end over the music.

She hangs up and sighs. 'That was my elderly neighbour – Mrs Fitzpatrick. She needs some help with something. Again. When she couldn't get hold of my mum, she asked if I'd go over. She always does this. Normally Mum goes, but now I'll have to. It's probably nothing but I can't just leave her.'

'Aren't you a bit drunk?' I say. 'Maybe I could go? I haven't had as much as you.'

'No, you stay,' Gabby insists. 'I won't be long. I'll slip out the back. If anyone asks, just let them know. I bet no one even notices I've gone. Will you keep an eye on Seffie for me? You're in charge while I'm out.'

'Wait a sec. What was it you wanted to talk to me about?'

Gabby turns back. 'What?'

'Earlier. Before everyone got here. You said there was something you wanted to tell me. I've only just remembered.'

'Oh, um, that was nothing. I can't even remember now.' Gabby opens the back door and disappears.

In the living room, Sasha finds Seffie has taken centre stage, dancing to 'I Wish It Could Be Christmas Every Day'. Only moments ago, Gabby had been doing the same thing, dancing as if no one was watching. Perhaps the sisters aren't so different after all; Sasha wishes Gabby could see that, and just let Seffie in.

No one is urging Seffie to go back to bed, and Sasha notices she's changed out of her pyjamas and is now wearing a sequinned silver dress. Then Sasha notices she also has on Gabby's dark red lipstick, making her look far older than ten.

Sasha rushes over to her. 'Seffie, what are you doing? If Gabby catches you here—'

'Oh, please, Sash, let me stay. Just for a bit.'

Sasha considers this request. What harm can a few minutes do? And Gabby isn't even here. 'Maybe just until the end of this song, then. But that's it. Straight to bed after that. Promise?'

Seffie throws her arms around Sasha. 'Thank you, thank you, thank you. I wish *you* were my sister.'

'You wouldn't say that if I actually was!' But Sasha's silently pleased. She's often wished she'd had a sister; despite her parents' best efforts, it was lonely growing up in a house that was absent of laughter and play.

'I just want to have fun,' Seffie says. 'Like Gabby always does. It's not fair that she's so much older than me. She can do whatever she wants. I wish I was older.'

Sasha's about to warn this child not to wish her life away, but Seffie is already dancing again, spinning around the room, a wide smile spread over her face.

Across the room, Shaun is deep in conversation with Anna, who appears to be giving him a lecture. And in the corner, Fin is discussing something with Andre, who every now and again glances at Seffie. She wonders what Andre and Seffie were talking about at the top of the stairs earlier, but brushes it off. Andre's a nice guy, he was just being kind to Seffie, like Sasha always is.

As soon as the song is over, Seffie tries to bargain, begging for one more song. But Sasha stands her ground; it's good practice if she wants to make a success of being a primary school teacher once her training's finished.

Sasha follows a reluctant Seffie upstairs, just to make sure she actually does go to bed this time, but she has a feeling this won't be the last time she sees Seffie tonight.

Outside her room, Seffie stops. 'Do you love Fin?' she asks.

Sasha smiles. 'Maybe. But don't tell him, will you?' Perhaps Fin already knows that she has feelings for him that extend beyond their friendship, but when she's ready to tell him it has to come from her, not any of their friends, or Seffie. Once again, she feels that giddy anticipation. So far tonight they haven't had a chance to talk. She needs to find him now.

'He is kind of cute,' Seffie says.

'And way too old for you to even think about,' Sasha warns.

'I know, I know. I'm just saying. You two are cute together. I hope you get married and have lots of kids. But with your hair, not his. Yours is nicer.'

'Well, thanks. I kind of do, too. Anyway, bedtime, young lady.'

Seffie laughs and closes her door. 'Good night, Sasha,' she calls.

Fin is coming out of the toilet when Sasha reaches the stairs. 'I was just thinking about you,' she says.

He smiles. 'You got Seffie to bed, then,' he says. 'See, you're already a great teacher.'

'Hardly. She'll probably be down again in a few.'

'We'd better disappear then, let someone else deal with it.' He takes her hand. 'Come with me.'

'Where are we going?'

'You'll see.'

They head to the kitchen. 'What are you—'

'Patience, Sash. I've got something to show you.' He opens the back door and they step into the garden. Even without their coats, she hardly feels the cold, despite the temperature being barely three degrees when the sun was out. Instead, Sasha's body feels warm, and a pleasant tingling sensation spreads through her. *It's because I'm about to be alone with Fin*, she thinks to herself.

But there's something else, too. Her head feels heavy, fuzzy around the edges. And she feels as though, somehow, she's detached from her body.

She wonders what's wrong with her. And then Fin leads her into the glass-fronted outbuilding that serves as Gabby's parents' garden office.

TEN

NOW

21:59

In my en suite, I lock the door and splash cold water on my face. My body is a furnace, despite the freezing temperature outside. With water dripping onto my dress, I sink to the floor, clinging to the side of the bath, and force myself to breathe deeply.

Seffie. The thought of her being dead crushes my skull, as it always does when this possibility seeps into my mind.

My memory of that night is hazy – small bursts of scattered conversations, flashes of my friends that disappear before they're fully formed. And none of it fits together into anything cohesive. My mind grapples with how they can think I could have killed Seffie. Yet they do. Even Fin, I'm sure, despite his assurances that he doesn't. And if I can't remember, then how can I say for sure it wasn't me?

If I'm responsible for something happening to Seffie, then Anna's right and the others have been protecting me all these years, by staying silent. It had been Anna who'd told me not to say anything, even to Gabby. And she'd vouched for me, telling the police that she'd been with me the whole evening.

And it had all been to protect my career. The teacher with so much promise. Sasha Hunt, who was destined to change lives.

I might be the one who changed Seffie's. Gabby's, too. All of our lives, but not in the way everyone imagined I would.

Someone knocks on the bathroom door.

'Are you okay?'

It's Andre. His voice is soft and calm, as it always was. An image forces its way into my head, a distorted vision of Andre, leaning in close to someone. Laughing. Flirting? And I'm observing from afar.

'Please open the door, Sasha. Talk to me.'

For a moment, I stay still. I could pretend I'm not in here and wait for him to leave, but I need to face this. Slowly, I open the door.

'We're all worried about you,' Andre says. 'You know Anna. She doesn't always have the most tactful way of expressing things.'

'Why are you here, Andre? If you all think I'm a murderer, then why are you concerned about me? Especially you. Those messages are... sometimes vile.'

Andre closes my bedroom door and sits on the chair by the window. 'Sash, I honestly haven't been sending you messages.'

He sounds so honest that for just a second I falter in my belief. But I know it's him. The tone of the messages, the way the sentences were formed. It's Andre all over.

'None of us knows what happened to Seffie,' he says. 'We didn't see anything. But when we went over it all, you were the last person to be with her. We'd all seen you. And all of us were accounted for. I was with Shaun – we were in the kitchen chatting about how we were spending Christmas Day. I was moaning about having to spend it with my family. And Anna and Fin took themselves to the off-licence as the drinks were running low.'

'And Gabby wasn't even there. So that just leaves me.'

Andre bites his lip. He always used to do this when he was feeling shy. Nervous. 'Do you really not remember? Even years later – has nothing come back to you?'

'No. It's all just a gaping black hole. There's nothing there. And nothing I can do will force it to the surface.' I don't tell him about the flickering images that often pop into my head. Seffie in her silver dress. Fin going to get me water. Then there is nothing. All I know is what they all told me the next day, and even that's hazy.

'Why have you been messaging me all these years?' I repeat. 'Some people would call it stalking. If you think I could be capable of killing someone, then why have anything to do with me?'

'Sasha, please don't do this. Do you want me to show you my phone? There'll be no messages to you. I don't even have your number.' Through his golden skin tone, his cheeks flush red. He's angry with me, but somehow keeping it silent.

'I'm sure I only had a couple of glasses. And no one remembers seeing me drinking more than that. There wasn't time. Yet, I blacked out.'

Andre frowns. 'I know. We wondered if you'd been on medication or anything. Some medicine mixed with alcohol can be dangerous.'

'I would never have done that. I was sensible, Andre. I was studying to be a teacher. I didn't even like drinking that much. And now I don't even touch it.'

'I noticed that,' he says. 'I didn't want to draw attention to it, though, in case you wanted to keep it low-key. I mean, we all changed after that night. I know I did.'

I think of all the messages Andre's sent me over the years. Some of them tender and thoughtful. As if we were in a relationship. Telling me about his day, as if I was reciprocating. And never once did I reply. But still they kept coming. And then they became aggressive. Accusatory. Laced with menace. As if there was a ticking time bomb next to me that I couldn't escape. Several times I'd even changed my phone number, but he always found a way to get my new one.

Andre will never admit that it's him. And if he's capable of sending those awful things, what else could he be capable of?

'No one changed more than Gabby,' I say. *Apart from the person who knows what happened to Seffie*, I think to myself. *How does anyone live with that?*

'Sash? What's wrong? You've gone all pale.'

Andre never calls me that. It was only Fin who used to shorten my name. Something about it doesn't feel right.

He takes my hand and I feel a flash of familiarity, even though I'm sure he's never done this before. 'Let me help you, please. We can work out together what to do about all this.'

Another flash of something. Familiar words I've heard Andre saying before. 'What did I say that night?' I ask. 'To you? Can you remember any conversation we had?'

He shrugs. 'We didn't really talk that much. Mostly you were with Fin. And you weren't being that coherent. But we all sorted it for you, Sash. We told the police you were sleeping it off and that Anna had been with you the whole time.'

'Why did you go along with that?'

'Because we were friends and we stuck together.'

I want to scream at him that it wasn't me, that I didn't need protecting because I would never have hurt Seffie.

'You were too spaced out to defend yourself,' Andre continues. 'But you trusted us then, so can't you trust me now? We need to stick to the story. Maybe it was a mistake not telling the truth back then about you having no memory of most of that evening. We should never have told the police you'd been passed out drunk the whole time, but it's too late now. And we'll all get into a hell of a lot of trouble if we change the story now. I think that's what Gabby's hoping will happen.'

I know Andre is right, but I'm not sure I want to continue this lie. And someone sent me the dress. 'Was that dress from you?'

'The Secret Santa gift? No. Why?'

'Seffie was wearing an identical one that night. Are you going to try and pretend you didn't notice?'

He frowns. 'Sorry, I don't pay much attention to clothes.'

This is all too convenient. How can I be the only one who remembers? 'Gabby was arguing with Shaun just now,' I say. 'About someone knowing where Seffie is. Which means she definitely knows we've been lying about my memory of that night.'

Andre takes a moment to answer. 'I think she knows too.'

'Why didn't you say anything?'

'I've been trying to just get my head around it. To be sure.'

Pounding on the door interrupts us. Before I can answer, it bursts open and Fin is standing there, out of breath. 'You have to come quick. It's Gabby!'

ELEVEN

NOW

22:07

Gabby's standing in the hallway shouting at Anna when Fin, Andre and I get downstairs. 'Get off me!' she yells. 'I don't need your help.'

Anna glances at us and shrugs. 'Come on, sweetie,' she says, turning back to Gabby. 'Let's go and rest.'

'That's what I've been doing for all these years!' Gabby screams. 'And it ends tonight.' She turns to us. 'So come on, then. Where is my sister? What happened to her? I know one of you knows. Look at you all. Pretending to be my friends, just like you did back then. Maybe you're all in it together! You all know what happened to her!'

Shaun tries to take her hand. 'Come on, Gabby. I know you're upset. It's Christmas, and it's bringing it all back. But we don't know where Seffie is. If we knew what had happened to her, we would have told you all those years ago. You know that, don't you?'

Gabby turns to him and pounds on his chest, screaming so loud the sound seems to echo through the hall. Since we got here she's managed to keep it together, but now she's falling apart. Silence descends on us, and even Gabby stares at Shaun as if she can't quite grasp that she's just attacked him.

More than anything, Shaun looks hurt by what's just happened. Which only makes me angrier. He has no right to be offended; he's lying to her about my blackout, as are we all.

'I think I see her sometimes,' Gabby says. 'I could be anywhere, and then I'll catch sight of her. In the street. In a park. And it's always a ten-year-old girl I see, never the twenty-two-year-old she'd be now. And it messes with this.' She taps the side of her head. 'Screws me up. I won't live like that any more. No one is leaving here until I know the truth. This snowstorm has been a godsend. But I would have found another way to keep you all here, if I'd had to. Whatever it takes. For my sister. I'll call the police if I have to. And I'll say whatever I need to say if it will make them reopen the investigation. Because I know one of you knows what happened to Seffie.'

I step forward and try to take Gabby's hand, but she pulls away. 'Don't touch me. Any of you. Just don't touch me.'

'Was my Secret Santa gift from you?' I ask. 'The dress.'

'No. But Seffie had one just like it. I'd forgotten all about it until you opened your present.'

My throat constricts. So it wasn't Gabby who gave me the dress. I cast my mind back, and amid the fog, I recall that Gabby had already left to go to Mrs Fitzpatrick's house when Seffie came downstairs wearing it. She'd begged me to let her stay downstairs to dance to just one song. Gabby had told the police Seffie was wearing her pyjamas, and none of her clothes were missing so she would have disappeared in them. But the rest of us saw Seffie in that dress.

'Why didn't you say anything when I opened the present?' I ask. I can't be sure she's telling the truth about my gift, and it's safer to assume she's lying.

Gabby's anger has defused, emptied out of her like air from

a balloon. Her shoulders sag and she sits on the bottom stair. 'I didn't remember Seffie had a dress like that until I saw it crumpled on the floor in your room. Then it came back to me. That morning she'd asked to wear it to my party, and of course I said no. I hid it in the back of her wardrobe.'

Gabby's words don't feel genuine – they're too rehearsed, like everything she's said since I got here. She's made it clear what she wants to do.

'Someone knows what happened to my sister,' she says.

It feels as though I'm weighed down by heavy stares. 'Gabby...' I begin, unsure how I'll ever find the words to tell her the truth, but knowing I have to do this.

'Come on,' Anna interrupts, taking Gabby's arm and pulling her up. She lolls to the side, but lets Anna lead her upstairs. 'Let's talk about this in the morning. Forget the party. Why don't we all get some rest and sleep off this alcohol. We've all had a lot, haven't we? We can talk through everything tomorrow. And it's Christmas Day tomorrow – we'll still need to eat.' She glances at me, her eyes flashing a warning to go along with this.

I watch them head upstairs. 'People have to pay for their actions,' Gabby moans. And we all stay silent.

When we hear the door shut upstairs, Shaun beckons us into the kitchen. 'Gabby's unstable,' he whispers. 'She's not going to drop this in the morning. And she'll be sober. What the hell are we going to do?' He turns to me. 'You can't tell her the truth, Sasha. Because then she'll know we've all lied to her. And worse, lied to the police. We've hindered their investigation. That's a serious offence.'

'So is murder!' I say.

Fin closes the kitchen door then takes my arm and ushers me into a chair. 'Think about this, Sash. She'll accuse you of having something to do with Seffie. It will open up a whole new investigation and you could lose your job.' He takes a deep breath. 'Let's just stay calm. We don't know what happened to Seffie. One minute she was in her room asleep, and then she was gone. None of us saw her. Telling the truth won't bring her back.'

A slick of bile sits in my throat. Was it me? Did I harm poor Seffie? I'm seconds away from throwing up. 'No,' I say. 'I need to tell Gabby the truth. I should have told her straight away. I can't let this carry on.'

'You'll lose everything you've worked so hard for,' Fin warns. 'You might even go to prison.'

He thinks it was me, he must do, otherwise he wouldn't be so adamant that I need to keep quiet. 'I don't care,' I say. 'Gabby deserves to know the truth. And maybe she'll—'

'What?' Shaun says. 'Tell you not to worry, and that it's okay? Are you out of your mind? She'll go straight to the police.'

'She can't – at least, not straight away. The roads are getting too treacherous, remember? No one will come out here for a while.'

Shaun shakes his head. 'Well, it's your funeral. Leave me out of it.'

'You just asked if I'm out of my mind,' I say. 'Yes, that's exactly what I am. What I have been all these years. And I want it to stop.'

Fin takes my hand. 'Just take a moment to think about this. We're all involved because we lied to the police. And Anna will be in trouble for being your alibi. We said you were asleep the whole time but you weren't, Sash. And if they find out we all covered for you, we're in serious trouble. Shaun has kids.'

'And a wife,' I say. 'Don't forget about his wife, sitting at home with those kids right now. Anyway, I can say I lied to all of you. Keep you out of it.'

Shaun frowns. 'That won't work. The whole point is that it will make them reopen everything.'

'I think Shaun's right,' Fin says, pleading with me. I still haven't told him what I witnessed Shaun and Gabby doing last night, and I force the memory from my mind. 'You've been very quiet,' I say to Andre. 'Why don't you add something? Normally you have a lot to say to me.'

Andre's eyes widen, a rabbit caught in headlights, and I immediately regret my words.

'Come on, Sash,' Fin says. 'Let's talk about this in the morning.'

I pull away from him and rush upstairs. I won't let them decide my fate this time. They were the ones who persuaded me to stay quiet about not remembering, otherwise I would have told the truth. I won't live in fear any longer. Once this is all out, I'll be able to breathe again. Stop holding my breath and waiting for the bomb to explode.

In my room, I close the door, wishing there was a lock on it. And I think about Seffie, with her whole life ahead of her. I would never have hurt her. I'd been happy to take her under my wing whenever Gabby was dismissive of her, wanting her out of the way. And all Seffie had wanted was to be acknowledged by the sister she looked up to.

Outside, the snowstorm continues relentlessly; even if Gabby calls the police tomorrow, it's unlikely they'll be able to get to us.

I change into my pyjamas and brush my teeth but it's so cold I grab one of Gabby's dressing gowns from the wardrobe and put it on before climbing into bed. Sleep won't come easily, not when tomorrow everything will change again. And Gabby will finally know the truth. I just have to be prepared to deal with the fallout.

02:46

My eyes open, blurry from sleep. Slowly, my vision clears and there's someone sitting on my bed, watching me.

Gabby.

I sit up. 'What's going on?' I reach for my phone: it's nearly three a.m.

'I know you're lying.' Her voice is calm and sober, and I'm relieved that she's at least slept off some of the alcohol. It was always easier to talk to Gabby when she hadn't been drinking.

'How long have you been sitting there?'

'I was just getting things straight in my head.'

I tell her I'm listening, and hold my breath while I wait for her to speak.

'You know by now I invited you all here because I wanted to find out the truth about Seffie.' She holds up her hand. 'And don't try to tell me that none of you knows what happened, because I know it's a lie. I *know*, Sasha.'

My throat constricts. I want to believe that I'm still asleep and this is a nightmare. Gabby isn't really here; she's sleeping in her bed.

'A few months ago, I got an email from a random address,' she explains. 'I don't know who sent it, but it was short. All it said was that one of my friends knows what happened to Seffie. That's it. Nine little words that went off like a bomb.'

I stare at her, trying to make sense of what she's telling me. Does someone else know what happened? None of us would have sent that email.

'I didn't say anything to any of you because you wouldn't have come, would you?' Her eyes fix on me. 'I replied to the email, asking who it was, but it bounced back. Whoever sent it must have deleted the account straight away.'

She waits for me to respond, but I can't find any words.

'So are you going to tell me, Sasha? Where is my sister?'

TWELVE
BEFORE

'What are we doing in here?' Sasha asks Fin, whose mischievous smile makes her hungry for him.

'I just wanted to be alone with you for a moment. Away from all the noise. Just us.' He takes her hand and they step inside.

'We shouldn't be in here. It's Gabby's dad's office.' Sasha looks around, taking in the rows of shelves lined with books. Normally, she'd rush to study them – Gabby's father is a philosophy lecturer, and she'd love to delve into the titles he chooses to fill his personal space with – but tonight, reading is the last thing on her mind. 'He might have private things in here,' she says.

'What, like porn?' Fin laughs. 'We won't need any of that.' He flashes that mischievous smile again. 'But if it makes you feel better, we won't touch anything in here. Look, there's a sofa. Come on.' He leads me to it and we flop down onto it, laughing. This feels forbidden. Dangerous.

A crushing pain sears through my head, forcing me to close my eyes and lean back.

'Sash? You okay?'

'Yeah. Fine.' But I can't open my eyes to see him; it feels better to keep them shut.

'You don't sound okay,' Fin says. 'Those cocktails Anna made were lethal, though. I'm a bit wasted.'

But Sasha doesn't remember having a cocktail. Just a couple of glasses of Prosecco. She may not be able to drink like Gabby, but two glasses have never floored her before. And she's sure that's all she's had. But at this moment, Sasha doesn't feel in control of herself at all. 'I think I need some water,' she says, pulling herself up. 'Is there anything in here?'

Fin looks around. 'Doesn't look like it. Just a computer and a ton of books. Files, too. I'll go and get you some from the kitchen.'

'Wait, come here.' Sasha pats the seat of the sofa and waits for him to sit again. 'When you come back, I think we should do it.'

Fin smiles. 'Do it?' Again, that cheeky grin she loves, where his eyes shine and he looks at her as if she's the only person in the world.

'Yeah,' she says. 'You know. Change everything. There'll be no going back after, though.'

Fin nods. 'That's fine with me. You weren't that good a friend anyway.'

'Hey!'

'I'm just kidding. We'll still be friends. That won't change.'

'Wait!' Sasha says. 'I've had second thoughts. This is too planned – I want it to be spontaneous.'

He laughs and kisses her forehead. 'Okay, then. How about this. I'll go and get you some water, and then when I come back, we can be spontaneous. As much spontaneity as you want. In fact, all the spontaneity!'

She prods his arm. 'Ha-ha, comedian. Please go and get me some water before I pass out. Then spontaneity will most definitely be off the cards.'

Fin salutes. 'Going right now, ma'am.'

When he's gone, Sasha rests her head back and closes her eyes again. But the crushing sensation is still there.

A few minutes pass and then she hears pounding on the door. Fin must have locked himself out. She stands up, and her head spins, so she sits down again. 'That was quick,' she says. 'I hope you've got a big glass – I could drink a whole gallon.'

'Sasha! Sasha!'

She jolts at the sound of Seffie's voice. She tries to get up again, but her legs won't support her weight. 'Seffie!' she calls.

'Sasha! Let me in! Something awful's happened!'

THIRTEEN

NOW

02:47

I stare at Gabby sitting at the edge of my bed; the accusation in her words makes my stomach cramp. There's a lopsided smile on her face, as if she knows what I'm thinking, and it's clear she believes she holds the upper hand. 'Why are you lying to me, Sasha? I want the truth.' She reaches into her pocket and I freeze. Gabby has always been unpredictable, but now more so than ever.

'I don't know what happened to Seffie. I'm sorry – I wish—'

Gabby's arm flies towards me and she grabs my wrist. 'You do know that I'd do anything to get to the truth? For my sister. I owe her that.' Her eyes narrow.

And even though her threat hangs between us, and the uncertainty of what she will do, I know that now is the time for the truth. 'There is *something* I need to tell you,' I say.

Gabby lets go of me and her hand moves back to her pocket. 'Go on.'

'That night. I... I don't remember anything that happened after Fin went to get me some water.'

She edges forward. 'What do you mean?'

'I think I blacked out. I was so out of it. Everything I remember is what the others told me. And they may as well have been talking about someone else, because I can't remember a damn thing.'

As I say this, a scene crashes into my mind: *Seffie running. Crying. Shouts calling after her. I'd never seen her run before – she hated any sport but gymnastics – but in that moment she was running for her life. Was it from me?*

Gabby's eyes widen. 'What the hell are you saying, Sasha?'

'I don't know what happened to Seffie. Because I can't remember anything. But I know it wasn't anything to do with me. I can't tell you how I know that, but I hope you'll trust me.'

For a few moments, my revelation hangs in the chilly air. And all the time Gabby just stares at me, her mouth moving as if she wants to talk but then nothing coming out. 'I set up cameras,' she says. 'Because I figured if what that email said is true, then sooner or later someone would slip up and reveal themselves. Especially with alcohol freely flowing.'

I should tell her that I know about the cameras, but the words lodge themselves in my throat. I need Gabby to trust me.

'But someone's turned them off,' she says. 'Proving that I can't trust any of you.'

And now I know I have to come clean; I can't let her think one of the others did it. 'Gabby, I—'

'But that's not the worst thing.' Gabby leans towards me. 'I have a notebook. It's got a detailed chronology, everything from that night. And I think I know who's responsible for Seffie's disappearance.'

'What? Who?'

Gabby ignores my question. 'You see, when you start asking questions, the same ones over and over, sooner or later people trip up.' She edges back. 'Someone's taken my notebook, and it can only be one of you. I've searched the whole house and can't find it anywhere. But I kept it under my bed. The only place without CCTV. Which just proves that someone here is guilty.'

'I haven't got your notebook,' I say. 'I swear—'

'I know you haven't. I narrowed down the time it went missing and I could see where you were.'

I think of Anna, how I caught her rummaging through Gabby's things, right before I turned off the cameras.

'I need help,' Gabby continues. 'And I'm putting my trust in you because I know how you always were with Seffie. You always had time for her. Patience. Kindness. That's not someone who would hurt her. Make her disappear. Not someone who would cover something up.' She stares at me. 'Maybe you're the one who sent me that email in the first place.'

I shake my head. 'That wasn't me. And how do you know you can trust it?'

'Because what would anyone have to gain by sending it? And do you know how sick it makes me feel that one of you could have hurt Seffie?'

I want to reach for Gabby, but I'm convinced she'll push me away, so I don't move.

She looks up again, her eyes glistening. 'Don't you realise that you're being lied to as much as I am, Sasha?'

I don't say anything, but I've felt this too. 'Because of the dress.'

Gabby nods. 'I didn't give it to you. Which means one of the others did. And why would they do that to you? I tried to find out from my friend which name she gave to each of you but she'd deleted the emails.' Gabby shakes her head.

'I got the wallet for Fin,' I say, remembering how much time I'd taken over choosing it. And for that hour I'd spent shopping, I'd allowed myself to pretend that this Christmas would be just about me and Fin, and everything that was unfinished between us. 'Who did you buy for?' I ask, switching off thoughts of Fin.

'The backpack for Anna.'

'Why did you bother with the Secret Santa thing? You didn't need to do it.'

Gabby smiles. 'I remember telling Seffie about it once and she loved the idea of it. She made us all do it the Christmas before. I wanted to do it this year for her.' A tear falls from her eye. 'Seffie adored you. You have to help me find that notebook, Sasha. Then I'm going to make someone pay for what happened.' She grabs my arm. 'Help me find out what happened to her. For your own sake as well as mine. We need to do this for Seffie.'

I nod, even though I'm still not sure I can trust Gabby.

'None of us is going anywhere,' she says, letting go of my arm. 'Not in these treacherous conditions. None of you know what it feels like, do you? To be trapped in a snowstorm with no idea of when you'll be able to leave. Knowing even if you call the police, help won't come any time soon.'

It's hard not to read her words as a warning, despite her assuring me that she trusts me.

'I need that notebook, Sasha. And the person who took it is the one who knows what happened to Seffie.' She lowers her voice. 'The one who did something to her.'

'And then what? What exactly are you planning to do?'

'I'm going to force them to confess.' Gabby smiles. 'Not too difficult when there's no escape from here, and I'm the only one who knows this area. I could find my way anywhere around here blindfolded, even in the snow.'

'I'll help you try to find that notebook,' I say.

She nods. 'Like I said, every tiny detail about what happened that night is in there. Timelines. Places everyone claimed to be. Everything I remember people saying or doing.'

'Wouldn't the police have already gone through all that?'

'Yes, twelve years ago. But I've kept it fresh in my mind. I bet none of the same officers are even still working in the same jobs. No one's as invested in this as me. And maybe when we find it, going through it might trigger a memory in you? Memory's a strange thing. Like I said, there are inconsistencies in what people said at the time.' Gabby shakes her head. 'Other than your massive lie, of course, Sasha. For starters, Anna wasn't with you then. So where was she? We need to find out from her.'

I nod, but feel a flicker of doubt. What if there's something I don't want to remember? What if it all points to me?

'It's Christmas Day, so people might let their guard down. I'll get the drinks flowing early to make sure of that.'

I frown. 'Is that a good—'

'Don't worry – I won't touch a drop. I know I can get carried away. It's my way of dealing with all of this. Of dealing with all of you.'

Despite the harshness of her words, I understand. 'I know.'

Gabby doesn't leave until I promise again that I'll help her. And when she leaves, uneasiness floats around me.

There is a clock ticking, and I have no idea if I can trust Gabby. What if I'm the one she's trying to expose?

FOURTEEN
BEFORE

Anna watches Shaun, wondering yet again what Gabby sees in him. Yes, he's good-looking, in that *I'm handsome and I know it* way that Anna finds repulsive. He takes care of himself, though, which is something at least; his body is toned and he always smells nice. Anna laughs. Maybe he's good in bed. Gabby's addicted to the sex. That would explain it. But sooner or later, she's bound to see him for what he is. His shallowness. Immaturity. Not to mention all the women who have had a piece of him.

Another thing that's annoying Anna is these bloody Christmas songs. She's sick of them. She can't wait to get out of here and go travelling, if that's the path that's been laid out for her. Time will tell. Tonight she will be fully awakened, that's for sure. Then she'll know what turn her life is meant to take.

Fin and Sasha have snuck off to the garden office. Probably to finally sleep together – it's about bloody time. She hopes it's worth it after they've waited so long. What would Sasha do if it was just one big let-down? Anna smiles. That's so often the case with men. Or perhaps Fin will be the one who's disappointed. He's got the patience of a saint, that one. Anna would have ripped Sasha's clothes off long ago. Not that she's into Sasha like that. No way. She loves the girl, but that's as far as it goes. They're friends, and Anna will never cross that line.

She leaves Shaun talking to Andre and goes to the kitchen, looking out at the garden.

Shaun appears behind her. 'Hey, you seen Gabby?'

'Nope, not for a bit.'

'I wonder where she is.'

'Avoiding you?' Anna laughs. When his face falls, she adds that she's just kidding. Jeez, Shaun really has got it bad for Gabby, despite the queue of girls lining up for him.

Shaun frowns. 'She has been acting a bit distant tonight. Has she said anything to you?' He sits on a barstool and pours himself some wine. 'Want some?'

'Yep. Cheers.' Anna finds an empty glass and hands it to him. 'Fill me up,' she says, laughing.

She climbs onto the barstool next to him and rearranges her dress. It's low-cut and she's aware she's making it even lower by tugging on it.

Shaun's eyes briefly fall on her breasts but then he turns back to his drink, taking a large gulp.

'Slow down, Shauny. Otherwise you'll be in no fit state to... you know. Whenever you and Gabby can sneak off.'

'I've tried,' he says. 'She doesn't seem interested tonight. That's why I was thinking something's up with her.'

Anna strokes his leg. 'Don't worry. Who could resist you, Shauny?'

He almost spits out his wine. 'Are you... are you flirting with me, Anna?'

'What if I am?'

'But you're—'

'I'm into whoever I want to be into,' Anna says, sliding her hand to the front of his trousers. She begins to stroke him, but he pushes her hand away.

'Woah, what are you doing?'

Leaning back, she pulls the top of her dress down and takes his hand, placing it on her breast. She's not wearing a bra and the feel of his hand against her skin excites her, even though it's Shaun. It's the forbidden thing, it must be.

'No, Anna, stop. I mean, I'm flattered, really I am, but I love Gabby. I'd never...'

She places her finger on his mouth. 'Shh. I know you're enjoying this. I can feel how hard you are.'

Shaun grabs her wrist and shoves her away. 'Just stop. Jesus, Anna!'

He stands and grabs his glass, stalking off and leaving her alone with her shame.

And something much more than that.

Rage.

FIFTEEN

NOW

Christmas Day, 08:25

My legs feel heavy as I make my way downstairs, wondering who might be already down there. I've had such little sleep since I got to Loch View House, it's a wonder I can function at all. But at least I'm one step closer to the truth. My conversation with Gabby replays in my head. What will the notes she's taken reveal? Which one of us is a murderer? *It's not me, it can't be.*

Outside, it has finally stopped snowing, but it looks like at least a foot of snow has fallen, making it a certainty that we are not getting out of here any time soon. I check my phone, and once again there's no reception – and no way for me to check on Scratch.

Ignoring the bubble of nausea in my stomach, I turn my attention to the coffee machine, familiar to me now, and make a strong coffee, relishing the bitter aftertaste it leaves.

Fin's in the living room, and he smiles as I approach. 'Feels weird to say Happy Christmas,' he says.

'I know.' It hardly feels like Christmas, even with Gabby's

excessive decorations. I look through the window again. 'Have you seen it out there?'

Fin nods. 'Not looking good. And I'm starting to feel hemmed in.' He pauses. 'Are you okay after last night? I wanted to check on you but thought I'd give you some space. I remember you always hated being crowded when you needed to work through things.'

I'm touched that Fin remembers this about me. I tell him I'm okay, but stay quiet about my late-night conversation with Gabby, and how much she'd spooked me sitting on the edge of my bed like that. 'Everything feels wrong. Out of place.'

'I don't regret what we did the other night,' he says. 'I know this might sound crazy, but it feels like it was always meant to happen.'

'Fin, I could be a murderer.'

For a fraction of a second, he falters. 'I'll take my chances, if you will.' He smiles. Fin always had a way of making light of things as a means to distract people. But sometimes things shouldn't be ignored.

'I can't talk about *us* now, Fin. There's too much to deal with. Do you know how hard it is to live with this gaping hole? Not knowing what I was doing for all that time. Not ever fully being able to trust myself.'

Fin crosses to the window. The view of the loch is still breath-taking, despite the snow. 'It's awful, I can imagine. But you can't let it stop you living.'

'Tell me again what you remember me doing that night, Fin. All of it.'

'I don't see what good—'

'Please, just humour me. What do you remember?'

Fin takes a deep breath. 'We'd been flirting all evening, like we always did – but there was the sense that something would finally happen that night. You'd split up with that guy you were with. Eamon, wasn't it? We were both single for the first time since we'd met.'

I nod. I'd been so excited to be alone with Fin. So excited that finally we were both free to be together.

'We snuck out to the garden office,' he continues. 'But you had a headache. You insisted you hadn't had that much to drink, but no one was keeping track, so who knows?'

I know. I didn't drink that much. I wanted to be in full control when Fin and I finally slept together.

'Then I went to get you some water.'

'And when you came back, I was crashed out on the sofa.'

Fin doesn't answer, turning back to the window, to the calming view of the loch.

'What is it?'

Seconds tick by before he responds. 'I... I'm sorry. I lied to you, Sasha. When I got back with your water... you weren't there.'

I stare at him. 'What? But—'

'I told everyone that's where I found you, but... I lied.'

My body freezes as I struggle to make sense of Fin's words. He doesn't look at me, but buries his head in his hands.

'Just tell me what the hell you're saying!' I demand.

'You weren't in the garden office. And you weren't in the house. I went to look for you and I found you out in the woods behind the garden. You were just roaming around, completely out of it. I took you back and that's when you crashed out on the sofa. I didn't tell anyone where I'd found you, because that's when Gabby came back and noticed Seffie was gone. None of this means you did anything. The police searched those woods and didn't find anything to suggest Seffie had been there. Not a thing. So I kept quiet. And then once I'd lied, how could I take it back?'

The horror of Fin's words fully sinks in, and I pummel my

fists into his chest. 'You should have at least told me! Why didn't you tell me?'

He takes hold of my wrists. 'Because you were already scared about not remembering anything. You know, in the days after, before we all agreed to not contact each other. You were distraught, wondering what had happened. I loved you, Sasha, I couldn't bear to see you in pain. I know it was wrong – I should have been honest with you – but if you'd known you'd gone into the woods then you would have been convinced you'd done something.'

My head spins. 'What was I doing out there? Gabby and I had gone for a walk earlier with Seffie. But why would I go back there? Didn't the police find traces of mud on my shoes?'

Fin sighs. 'You'd taken your shoes off earlier in the evening, remember? You said they were hurting. And I washed your feet when we got back, with some hand wipes that were on the desk. They were caked in mud and I didn't like seeing you like that.'

'Seffie,' I say softly. 'What happened to her? Did I—'

'No! You've got to stop thinking that.'

'Then who was it? She's dead, Fin, she has to be.'

We're interrupted by Shaun strolling into the living room. 'Morning. Happy Christmas. Am I disturbing something?'

'No,' I say. 'I was just about to have a shower.' And I need to process the information I've just learned from Fin.

Shaun stops me at the door. 'I hope you've had a rethink about yesterday? Telling Gabby you can't remember anything will open up a can of worms. We've all been covering for you, Sasha. Can't you just leave it?'

But it's too late. Gabby already knows, and together we'll work out what happened to Seffie. Even if the person I'll end up fearing the most is myself.

'Let's just get through today,' Fin says. 'Try to support Gabby. This isn't easy for her. Another Christmas where she has no answers about Seffie. Besides, what choice do we have? We're all stuck here now.'

Anna appears at the top of the stairs, tying her dressing gown belt. 'Is Gabby down there?' she asks. 'Didn't think she'd be up this early after the state she was in last night. But she's not in her bedroom or her bathroom.'

Gabby had sobered up when she came to my room. 'She's not down here,' I say.

Anna frowns. 'Oh, that's weird. Andre's having a shower but shouted that he hasn't seen her.'

Fin and Shaun appear in the hall. 'What's going on?' Shaun asks.

'Gabby's not in her room. Have either of you seen her?'

'No,' Fin says. 'And I've been up for a couple of hours. Couldn't sleep.'

I rush to the front door, which is locked from the inside. Unlocking it, I peer outside. Gabby's Land Rover is still in the drive, covered in snow, exactly where it's been parked since I arrived here. And the snow on the ground is undisturbed. 'Well, she hasn't gone anywhere,' I say. A sinking hollowness swells in my stomach. Without a word, I check all the rooms downstairs. Gabby isn't down here, and there are no footprints at the back of the house.

'I'll check upstairs again,' Anna says, disappearing.

'Maybe us being here is too much for her after all,' Shaun says. 'She might have gone for some fresh air.'

'How can she have gone for a walk in this?' I say. 'There are no footprints anywhere.'

'That's true. But the snow was still falling until a few minutes ago,' Fin says. 'Could have covered them. Let's just give it a while. She'll be back. This is Gabby we're talking about. No doubt she's doing this on purpose.'

Fin has a point. But I know what the others don't – why would Gabby leave the house when the two of us are supposed to be searching for her notebook? *But would she still want me to help her if she knew Fin had found me in the woods?*

When Shaun tells us he's going to get dressed, Fin ushers me into the living room. 'What if she's done this on purpose? To spook us? She's already said one of us knows something about Seffie.'

'Gabby doesn't play games like that,' I say. 'That's not her style.' But even as I say this, I have doubts; none of us knows each other any more. What if her coming to my room last night was a ruse? It's possible that Gabby thinks I had something to do with Seffie's disappearance. It's what everyone else thinks. 'We have no choice but to see how this plays out,' I tell Fin.

09:37

I've just got dressed when Andre knocks on my door. 'I guess I should say Happy Christmas,' he says. 'Can I come in?' He glances behind him.

'I was just about to go downstairs.'

'Just for a second.'

Being alone with Andre unnerves me, but he's already closing the door and making his way to the chair, strewn with my clothes. He pushes them to the side.

'No sign of Gabby, then?' I ask.

He shakes his head. 'Bit weird, isn't it? Where would she go on Christmas morning?'

'What did you want me for, Andre?' I could do without this visit – I need to find Gabby.

If he's offended by my bluntness, he doesn't show it. 'All of us being here together,' he says, 'has made me think about Seraphina. Course it has. And that night. I... I wondered if you remembered the conversation we had? Before she went missing. You've never mentioned it, but... is it anything to do with you accusing me of sending you emails? It's just, I don't get why you think I am.'

I shake my head. 'I can't remember anything after Fin went to get me some water.' But there is something about Andre that night, something I can't retrieve, like so much else.

'You were really angry with me that night,' he says.

I study his face, searching for something.

And that's when I remember.

SIXTEEN
BEFORE

Andre likes to sit back and observe people, even when he's had way too much to drink. It's where he's most comfortable. Being the centre of attention is something he abhors. He doesn't get rowdy when he's had a few – no, he just sits back and watches everyone else.

Anna is flirting with Shaun, dancing around him in her slinky dress, and Andre wonders what she's playing at. And where's Gabby? Would Anna be doing this if she was here? Possibly. Anna has no boundaries.

Andre doesn't like girls like that. As friends, sure, but he'd never let one into his life on an intimate level. No, he wants purity. Innocence.

If he's honest with himself, he feels out of place with these people now. His *friends*. As if he doesn't quite fit them any more. Maybe he never did.

'Anyone need another drink?' Shaun asks, edging away from Anna.

Andre holds up his full glass. 'I'm all right.' He's hoping no one will notice that this is the same drink he's had since he got here.

'I will, sweetie,' Anna says, blowing Shaun a kiss and laughing. She holds out her empty glass to him and watches him leave. What *is* going on with those two?

Andre is baffled further when Anna immediately follows Shaun to the kitchen.

He leans back on the sofa. He wonders where Fin and Sasha have gone, but it's better if he doesn't think about that. He's lost in these thoughts when Seffie appears in the doorway again. She's still wearing that silver sparkly party dress but at least the grotesque lipstick has disappeared. 'All I Want For Christmas' starts playing, and Seffie dances. She knows every word so she sings along, too, knowing any second now Andre will order her upstairs.

'Seraphina – what are you doing?'

'Dancing. What does it look like?'

Andre can't help smiling – she's got him there. He'd forgotten that kids take everything so literally. 'You need to go back to bed. If Gabby finds you down here, she'll—'

'My sister's not here. She left. She went to Mrs Fitzgerald's. She's always needing help with something. Forgetting where she's put things. Mum's always going over there.'

So that explains why no one's seen Gabby for a while. 'Come on,' Andre says. 'I'll take you up. Make sure you actually get there.'

'Can I just stay till the end of this song?' Seffie begs. 'Sasha let me earlier.'

He rolls his eyes. 'Fine. Then bed.'

When the song finishes, Andre ushers Seffie upstairs. 'There you go,' he says when they reach the top. 'There's your bedroom. How about trying to stay in it tonight? Don't you know how important sleep is?'

'Oh please, Andre. Can't I just stay downstairs until Gabby comes back?' She flashes a smile that it's hard to say no to.

But he gives it a good go. 'No.' He should say it more firmly or she'll sense his weakness.

'I'm scared,' Seffie says. 'I don't like being in my room with the door shut. I always sleep with it open but Gabby said I have to keep it shut. But I keep hearing noises.'

He rolls his eyes. 'Seraphina, that's just us downstairs.'

'I'm *scared*, Andre.'

He's no expert, but isn't ten a little old to still fear the dark? He glances downstairs. 'Fine. How about I check your room. Make sure it's all safe? And then you'll stay in it, right? And go to sleep?'

Seffie beams. 'Deal!'

Her room is large, and way too pink. But it's tidy, and Andre likes that. His flat is immaculate, and he's grateful he doesn't have to share it with anyone. He walks over to the window and peers through the blind. 'So you said Gabby's at that house across the road? Did you see her going inside?'

Seffie jumps on the bed and crosses her legs, clutching an oversized cuddly cat to her body. 'Yep. Mrs Fitzpatrick's house. She's like a hundred and ten or something.'

'We all grow old, Seraphina,' Andre says.

'Why do you call me that? No one does. Apart from Gabby when she's angry. I'm Seffie.'

'Seraphina sounds more grown up,' Andre says. 'I thought you wanted to be grown up. That's why you keep coming downstairs, isn't it?'

She shrugs. 'I just want to be like Gabby. She's beautiful. And confident. Everyone loves her. But I'm not like her.' She tilts her head and stares at Andre. 'I bet *you* like her, don't you?'

Andre takes his time to answer, because speaking his truth will change everything. 'No, I'm not interested in your sister.'

'Hmm. All men are.'

Andre leans forward and whispers, 'Want me to tell you a secret, Seraphina?'

SEVENTEEN

NOW

09:38

I stare at Andre, at a face that should feel familiar and comforting, yet somehow terrifies me. A closed book I cannot hope to read. He always was. 'It was about Seffie, wasn't it? I was shouting at you about her.' But why? She searches for the full memory but can't retrieve it.

Andre raises his eyebrows. 'You do remember, then.'

'Yes,' she lies. If she keeps him talking he might reveal something important, something she needs to hear to set herself free. Andre and Seffie. There's something there she can't grasp, wisps of smoke evaporating as she reaches for them.

'I didn't do anything to her,' he says. 'It wasn't what you thought. I don't know what you were thinking, but you nearly broke my jaw.'

I nod. How much longer before he realises I don't know what he's talking about?

'What you accused me of. I would never have hurt Seraphina in any way. Why would I?'

'She... she came to get me. She told me something awful had

happened.' My words take me by surprise; I have no idea whether they're true or not. I stare at him. There was blood on Seffie's door that no one could explain. Andre has been lying. 'You... hurt Seffie. You did that to her.'

He frowns. 'No, it wasn't like that. It was an accident. She was messing around, trying to go back downstairs. I put my arm out to stop her and my watch must have caught on her face, and she was bleeding. It was only a small amount. And you saw her after that. I had nothing to do with her disappearing. I was just trying to get her to stay in her room. I didn't do anything to her.'

'You didn't tell anyone that you took her to her room! That you were alone with her.'

'Because I know how it looks. And I think Gabby knows I lied. Last night I talked to her in the kitchen and she was asking me all these questions about that night. I could tell she didn't believe me.'

'Andre, do you know where Gabby is?'

'No. But I was hoping to clear the air with her this morning.'

'The truth will come out, Andre. I think we all know that, don't we? There's nowhere else for any of us to hide.'

11:04

We search the house for Gabby, separately so that we can cover more areas, but there's no sign of her.

'Did anyone check the garage?' I ask. 'If not, I'll go.'

'I did,' Shaun says. 'She's not hiding out in there.'

'Her coat and boots are missing,' Anna declares, slumping onto the sofa. 'Isn't that proof she's gone somewhere on purpose?'

All of us are silent, lost in our own thoughts. Gabby has been playing games with us since before we arrived at her house, so it's likely this is part of another one. Still, I can't help but worry – beneath her anger and pain, she'd seemed genuine last night.

What Andre told me has also disturbed me, but it's still not proof he knows what happened to Seffie. And he's not the only one of us who has lied.

Anna stands. 'I don't want to sit around here like this. Come on, let's get some food on or something. Gabby will turn up when she turns up. She must have neighbours she knows around here – maybe she's gone to see one of them?'

'On Christmas Day? That doesn't seem likely. And aren't you worried about her?' I ask.

Anna scowls. 'Why do you think I've spent all morning looking for her? And actually, this is Gabby we're talking about. Who told us she wanted us here to help her move on but has done the complete opposite! Asking us questions about that night, going on and on about it. It's not healthy. So, yes, I actually think Gabby is fine. She's just teaching us a lesson for... for who knows what reason? Maybe she's doing this because Seffie disappeared. I don't know! She's not exactly stable, is she?'

'Neither would you be if you'd lost your sister,' I say. 'And we all know what lesson Gabby's trying to teach us. We're liars!' I turn to Andre, who stares at me.

Fin comes over to sit beside me. 'Sasha,' he says, taking my hand.

I wait for him to say more, but he doesn't, gripping my hand tightly. And across the room, Andre watches us.

Shaun jumps up and paces the room, his trainers squeaking on the tiled floor. 'I think Anna's right and we should eat something,' he says. 'It is Christmas. And Gabby will be back soon – I know she will.' He smiles, as if trying to convince himself of this.

'Don't your wife and kids mind you being away from them for Christmas?' I ask.

'Alia understands why this was important.'

'Come on, Sasha,' Anna says. 'Will you come and help me?' She grabs my arm before I can object.

'I'm really not hungry,' I say, once we're alone in the kitchen.

'I want to get out of here,' she says. 'There's something going on and I don't understand it. This isn't what I came for. And where the fuck is Gabby? She's planned this – I know it. I can't be here, Sasha.'

I point to the window, at the solid blanket of snow covering the ground. 'None of us can go anywhere, can we?'

Anna clutches her head, as if she's in pain. 'Shit. I should never have come. I don't even like Christmas! But I came for Gabby. And now she's not even bloody here. Listen, there's something—'

'Thought I'd come and help.' Andre strolls into the kitchen.

'We're okay,' Anna says. 'It's all under control.'

Andre glances at the empty work surfaces. 'Happy to help. What are we doing?' He glances at the bread on the worktop. 'Sandwiches?'

'I thought we could save the roast for when Gabby gets back,' I say. 'We can have it this evening.'

'Whatever you say,' Andre says. He opens up cupboards and the fridge, gathering cheese and ham and whatever else he can find.

In all the time I've known Andre, I've never once seen him preparing food for anyone.

20:12

We attempt to venture out after lunch, calling for Gabby, our voices echoing into the bleak white landscape. Fin checks for shovels to try and clear a path, but he comes back empty-handed. 'Nothing,' he says. 'Which is bizarre, given that snow-storms must be common around here.'

'She's laughing at us,' Shaun says. 'I'm telling you – she's planned this.'

None of us responds.

Later, while the others sit downstairs in the living room, all of them with drinks in their hands, I slip upstairs. Listening out for their voices, or the sound of footsteps, I quickly root through each of their rooms. I feel no guilt for this invasion of privacy – I'm only doing what I must.

There's no time for a prolonged search, but after a scan through the rooms, there's no sign of any notebook.

By the time evening sets in, there's still no trace of Gabby. Unable to bear sitting around waiting, I head upstairs to my room, where at least I'll have some privacy. I don't know what the others will do now, but it's becoming apparent that none of us want to be around each other.

I've lost count of the number of times I've tried to call Gabby's phone – as have the others – and mostly there's no signal, but on the rare occasion it goes through, I'm greeted by her voicemail message. It's eerie hearing her voice in her own home, when there's no sign of her.

I leave a futile message. *Gabby. What's going on? Where are you? Please message me.* My phone pings, and for a fraction of a second I let myself believe that it's Gabby finally replying. It's from Jarred, though, wishing me a Happy Christmas, telling me he misses me and Scratch. I try to reply, but the signal drops and my message remains unsent.

A knock on my door startles me. I rush to answer it, hoping it's Gabby, but it's Fin standing there, holding out a plate of the sandwiches we made earlier. 'I thought you might be hungry. Sorry it's not turkey,' he says. 'Don't think any of us would be able to face that. I don't know about you, but after what happened with Seffie, I could do without Christmas. Ravinder loved it, though. It was a real bone of contention between us.' He hands me the plate.

'Thanks.'

'Mind if I come in?'

I want to say no, that I need to be alone, but somehow Fin's presence comforts me. We sit together on the bed, and his voice fills the silent void while I force down the cheese sandwich he's brought me.

When I've finished eating, he moves my plate away and kisses my neck. I let him for a moment – even though it feels wrong to do anything like this when Gabby's missing – but then I pull away. 'You know this could never work, don't you?'

'Please don't say that.' He strokes my cheek, pulls a lock of hair away from my eye.

'There would be that question hanging over us,' I say. 'You know there would. Especially now I know you found me wandering in the woods. One day you'd wake up and it would eat away at you. Did I kill Seffie? Every time we had an argument, it would emerge.'

'You're wrong, Sash. We don't even know that she's dead. They never found her body. She must have run away.'

'But the question is still there. And there was blood.' Which I don't tell Fin was because of Andre.

Tears glisten in Fin's eyes. 'Please give us a chance. I never stopped loving you. I know it doesn't make rational sense, but I feel it in here...' He thumps his chest. 'That you didn't do anything. You were in no fit state.' He takes my hand. 'You could barely walk straight, let alone do anything to Seffie. Listen, we could go somewhere. Another country. Like Anna did. She said it really helped her to forget. We could do the same – together. You could teach anywhere and I'd easily get work. Please think about it. As soon as we can leave here, we can start making plans.'

Fin paints a tempting picture. It would be so easy to run away from everything with him. But I need to know what happened. 'I can't,' I say. 'I've always loved you, but we can't be together.' Forcing back tears, I turn away. 'I'm sorry.'

Fin sighs and kisses my hand. 'I'm sorry too.' He stands. 'I'll leave you alone.'

As soon as the door closes, I turn off the bedside lamp and, fully clothed, pull the covers over me. I can't deal with my feelings for Fin right now. But I know what I do need to do.

02:17

I open my door a crack and listen. There's nothing but eerie silence, as if I'm alone in this sprawling house. I count to sixty, then, guided by the torch on my phone, make my way towards Gabby's bedroom.

Opening the door, I half expect her to be lying in bed asleep, and the sight of her neatly made empty bed chills me. *Where are you?*

I need to find Gabby's notebook. If she was even telling the truth about having one.

Even though there's no chance of it being in here if Gabby is right and someone's taken it, I root through her dressing table drawers, and recall catching Anna doing the same thing. She admitted being a kleptomaniac, but was she lying? Was she looking for Gabby's notebook? We're all shrouded in lies and I can't trust anyone. *Maybe even myself.*

After a thorough search of Gabby's room, I find nothing that could reveal where she is, or what she's planned, and no sign of any notebook.

I tiptoe out and make my way downstairs to Gabby's study, checking every cupboard and drawer, scanning the books on the shelves, in case she's slipped the notebook between any of them.

There's nothing.

In the kitchen, I pull out drawers and rummage through

cupboards, but my hopes fade fast when once again there's nothing to be found.

I look through the side door to see if the snow might have stopped, but it continues to fall, dashing my hopes of getting out of here any time soon. Opposite the house is the garage, with a half-cleared path leading up to it. Shaun will have done it when he went to check in there earlier. It occurs to me that the garage could be an ideal place for someone to hide Gabby's notebook.

Slipping on a pair of Gabby's boots that have been left on the mat, I follow the path Shaun has cleared. I'm dressed only in jeans and a jumper, and the cold air assaults me as I make my way to the garage door. I hold my breath as I reach for the handle, half expecting to find it locked. But Shaun hadn't mentioned needing a key to get in.

It opens, and I step inside, using my phone to search for a light switch. I press it and stark yellow light fills the room, forcing me to blink as my eyes adjust.

Cardboard boxes line the far length of the wall, and other than a tool shelf and a bike that looks brand new, there's nothing in here.

Making my way towards the boxes, my eyes are drawn to something on the floor, sticking out from behind a box.

Only when I get closer do I see that it's a sock. Puzzled, I lean down, almost falling over when I realise that I'm looking at not just a sock, but someone's foot, and it's hidden under a blanket. With nausea bubbling in my throat, I pull back the blanket, and find myself staring at Gabby.

She's sprawled on her back, her legs twisted behind her body, and her vacant eyes stare at the ceiling.

The teal scarf she received as a Secret Santa present is knotted tightly around her neck.

EIGHTEEN

NOW

03:29

Stifling the scream that's desperate to escape my mouth, I tug at the scarf to try to untie it. But it's too secure, and it takes what seems like an eternity for me to loosen it. I pull it away and gasp when I see the dark mauve ring it's made around her neck.

And then I turn and vomit all over the concrete floor. I check Gabby's pulse but there's nothing, and her arm is flaccid in my hand. Instinctively, I pull her up and hug her close to my chest, my tears soaking her dress. The same dress she was wearing when she came to my room last night.

I sit with her for several minutes, cradling her like a baby, before I can bring myself to move. Placing her back down gently, as if she's asleep, I make her a silent promise to find out who did this to her. And to find out what happened to Seffie.

At least this time I know it wasn't me, and it cements in my mind that it wasn't me who was responsible for Seffie's disappearance either.

As I make my way back to the house, the blizzard thrashing

down against me, my mind whirrs with one thought: *I'm not safe here.*

Inside, I head to Fin's bedroom, knocking on his door but not waiting for a reply before I open it.

He stirs and sits up when he realises I'm standing in his room. 'Sash. Are you okay? What's going on?' He glances at his watch.

The words don't want to leave my mouth. 'I've found Gabby.'

'Oh, good. Is she okay?'

'She's dead, Fin! I found her and she's dead!'

He jumps out of bed. 'What do you mean? She can't be!'

'You have to come.'

Fin follows me to the garage, but when we get there, he insists on going in first. 'It must have all been too much for her,' he says, before we step inside. 'Poor Gabby.'

'You don't understand,' I say. 'She didn't do this to herself.'

We step inside, and I look away while Fin takes in the scene. 'What the... Jesus!' He clamps his hand to his mouth.

'She was strangled. The scarf was wrapped around her neck! It was so tight I struggled to get it off.'

'You mean you touched her?'

'I had to! I didn't know if she was dead – I was trying to help her!'

Fin wraps his arms around me. 'I know. It's just... Look, it's okay.'

I howl into his chest. 'What the hell, Fin? Who did this?'

'I don't know. But we need to get out of here. We should never have come, but I had to see you, even if it's the last time.' He walks to the garage door, kicking at a snowdrift, as fierce wind howls around us. 'Fuck!' he yells. 'What the hell are we supposed to do?'

'There's only one thing we *can* do. We need to call the police.'

He pulls out his phone and taps on it. 'No reception,' he says, holding it out to me.

'Shit!' I try my own phone, and it's the same story. 'Even when we can get hold of them – what if they think it was me? I'm the one who found her.'

'Or me,' Fin says. 'But it wasn't us, so we have nothing to worry about. Other than that there's a murderer in the house.' He turns back to Gabby's beautiful house, which in the darkness only looks sinister. 'I don't like this,' Fin continues. 'What if it's you next? Or me? What if whoever did this to Gabby thinks they have to silence us all? They might be worried we know something. Maybe Gabby found something out?'

Fin's words echo my own thoughts.

'You know,' Fin says, 'sometimes I've wondered if it was Gabby who did something to Seffie. They were always arguing. What if they'd had a fight or something?'

'But we saw Seffie after Gabby had gone to the neighbour's house. Unless she came back unnoticed, it couldn't have been her.'

Fin points to Gabby; somehow, her wrecked and lifeless body still looks beautiful. At peace. 'Now I know it wasn't her,' he says. 'Come on, Sash, we really need to get back in the house and work out what the hell we're going to do.'

Slowly, I follow him back inside. 'All I know is, I'll do whatever it takes to find the truth. I've lost twelve years of my life and I won't live like this any more.'

Fin stops walking and turns to me. 'What are you saying?'

It takes me a moment to organise my thoughts, but then I'm completely clear. 'We can't tell anyone that we've found Gabby.'

'What? That's crazy!'

'I know how it sounds but hear me out. Once—'

'Jesus, Sasha, no. No way.'

'Just listen! Once the others know we've found Gabby, it

raises the stakes. Whoever killed her will be forced to make another move. And we're all trapped here. The murderer can't just go home and back to their life, hoping no one will ever find Gabby, or that it won't be traced back to this Christmas get-together. But if we keep quiet, he or she might get complacent. Do or say something that gives them away. And it buys us time to keep trying to get hold of the police. Remember, even if we can get through to them, it could be days before they can reach us.'

'This is insane!' says Fin.

'We don't have a choice, do we? Not when we're cut off in this godforsaken place.'

Fin stares at me, shaking his head. 'I can't... it's not right. We can't just leave her here and carry on as if nothing's happened.'

I take his hand, pulling him close to me. 'Do you have an alternative?'

Fin is silent, the only sound out here the howling wind. I glance back at the garage, where I can still see the heel of Gabby's foot. 'She won't have to stay here long,' I say. 'I've checked the weather again and the snow should ease up over the next couple of days. The police will be able to get to us then. And we'll be free to get away from here.'

Fin kisses the top of my head. 'If we find out who did this, and you clear your name, do you think there'll be a chance for us?'

I hate lying to Fin, but I need him to go along with this. 'It's the only way we might have a chance,' I say.

He exhales a deep breath. 'Okay, then. But I don't like it, Sash. Not one bit.'

07:48

If there was any doubt in my mind that Seffie is dead, there isn't now. Her body might never have been found but I've stared at

Gabby's, touched her lifeless flesh. And sat side by side with death.

And now the stakes are higher, and there's a tightness in my chest, as if fear has got me in a vicelike grip.

Before I went to bed last night I snuck into Gabby's bedroom to check if she'd switched the cameras back on. If she had, the question would have been answered and I'd know who to watch out for before the police can get here. I still can't get a signal, but I have to trust that it's only a matter of time before I do.

But Gabby hadn't touched the cameras, and, other than me, nobody knows about them, not even Fin – I'd forgotten to mention them to him. Even though I regret turning them off now, they could still come in useful.

Outside my room, I hesitate. Listening. Waiting. Then I slip into Gabby's room, heading straight to her walk-in wardrobe. The infrared CCTV cameras show me that everyone is still asleep. My stomach clenches. Which of these people, who I consider my friends, did that to Gabby? And where's it going to end?

In the kitchen, I make coffee, just for something to focus on, to keep me awake, because the thought of falling asleep terrifies me. I stare at the garage, my pulse racing. Playing this game, pretending I don't know what's happened to Gabby, is going to be hard to pull off, but what choice do I have?

My stomach rumbles; I barely ate yesterday so I'll need something to stop myself feeling faint. All my strength is required to face what's coming.

I'm surprised when Anna appears, still in her short pyjamas. 'No sign yet?'

'No.' The word lodges in my throat.

'Are you okay?' she asks. 'You disappeared to your room all evening.'

'Didn't feel much like Christmas, did it.'

She nods. 'It hasn't for twelve years, has it.' She gestures to my cup. 'Guess you don't want another one.'

'Only just made this.' I lift my cup, force coffee down.

She sets about boiling the kettle, throwing a teabag into a mug. 'At least have that down here with me,' Anna says. 'Don't take it to your room.'

I smile. 'Wasn't planning to.'

We sit at the kitchen island, cradling our mugs for warmth, and I make sure I'm facing away from the door, away from the garage where Gabby lies.

I put down my cup and stare at Anna. Now it's even more crucial that I find Gabby's notebook. 'You've been wanting to tell me something,' I say. 'You don't really steal things, do you? So are you going to tell me what you were doing in Gabby's room?'

NINETEEN
BEFORE

Gabby's beginning to regret having this party. Shaun can tell something's wrong, and she's finding it hard to keep up the pretence. And bloody Seffie. She just won't go to bed, and it's driving Gabby mad. And now the little brat is threatening to tell their parents all about the party when they get back from France. Her dad will hit the roof. Gabby didn't even bother trying to explain to him about this get-together she'd planned. Her father still seems to think she's a teenager who will arrange a raucous gathering of strangers in their house – in *his* house – and he wouldn't have stopped to listen if she'd pointed out that these are her close friends. None of them rowdy. All of them trustworthy. Gabby didn't need the grief – he's already threatening to throw her out. Because she's reckless. Drinks too much. Parties too hard. And where's it got her? She doesn't even know who she is any more. But she knows what she doesn't want. At least there is that.

There's something up with Andre tonight, too. He's acting weird, but she can't put her finger on why. She'll talk to him about it later – she likes Andre. How he listens more than he talks. So different from her.

Her phone rings – it's Mrs Fitzpatrick from across the road. She should answer it, but for some reason she presses the red button, and the ringing stops. She'll call her back. She's too much of a mess to speak to her now.

There's a knock on the door and without waiting for Gabby to answer, it opens and Anna is smiling at her, holding out a glass. 'And what are you doing, hiding in here? Thought you might want this.' She comes in and sits on Gabby's bed, handing her the drink. She's sloshed already, and the thin strap of her dress has fallen down her arm.

'I had a call from my neighbour,' Gabby says. 'She wants me to go over there urgently.'

'Really?' Anna says, frowning. 'But you're too pissed.' She lies back on the bed and stretches out her arms. 'Shaun's looking for you.'

Gabby's cheeks flush. 'Oh.'

'I told him you were sorting Seffie out. That shut him up for a while. Sorry about that.'

Gabby groans. 'I love Shaun,' she says.

Anna laughs. 'No, you don't.'

'Yes, I do.'

Pulling herself up, Anna cups Gabby's face and kisses her, sliding her tongue into Gabby's mouth.

Gabby pulls away. 'No. Get off me! I told you, it's over. We're not doing that any more. I made a mistake.'

Anna shakes her head. 'No. A mistake is a one-time thing. I've lost count of how many times we've slept together.' She places her hand on Gabby's thigh.

'Stop!' Gabby pushes her hand away.

'Get over it,' Anna says. 'I told you I'd back off and then you turned up at my house in the middle of the night, smiling sweetly in your skimpy shorts. What the hell are you playing at? And don't give me any of that shit about being confused.'

Gabby doesn't have the heart to tell Anna that she'd been

drunk that night. Just needed some company and Shaun was out. 'I'm not confused,' Gabby says. 'I just don't want to do it any more. It was supposed to be fun. You said you didn't like relationships. With men or women. But now look at you. You just won't let me go, will you?'

Anna looks hurt, and Gabby wishes she could take back her words. She cares about Anna. They're friends. It was supposed to be just messing around. Gabby had been drinking, of course, but after that first time, when she'd sobered up, she'd regretted it. Gabby loves Shaun. Yet Anna had been persistent, and Gabby had given in several more times.

But Anna was never supposed to get attached. This was *Anna*. What the hell had happened?

'What would Sasha think if she knew?' Anna says.

Gabby knows with a hundred per cent certainty what Sasha would think. That Gabby is scum for cheating on Shaun. But Gabby wanted to tell her earlier, when she and Sasha had been alone. To unburden herself about what a deceitful person she is. And how she's destabilising the bedrock of their friendship by sleeping with everyone.

Gabby gets off the bed and looks out of the window. 'I have to go,' she says. 'End of conversation.' She's aware of how callous she sounds, and when she turns back to Anna, expecting to see sadness on her friend's face, all that radiates from it is hatred.

TWENTY

NOW

07:56

Anna stares at me, then down at her coffee. 'You're right, I was lying about that. I don't steal things. Never have. I'm many things, but a thief isn't one of them.'

'Then what were you doing in Gabby's room?'

Anna doesn't look at me, and picks at her bright red nail polish.

'You better start talking, or I'm calling the police.' I don't point out that I've already been trying.

'The police? Why? I haven't—'

'What were you doing in Gabby's room?' I repeat. If this had been years ago, I would never have spoken to Anna like this. Now, though, she is a stranger to me.

'First, I need to explain about that night at the party,' Anna says. 'When Seffie went missing. I didn't know where Gabby was, so I'd gone looking for her. Found her in her room, avoiding Shaun.'

'Why would she have been avoiding Shaun? They were together.'

Anna sighs. 'They'd had an argument a few days before. You won't remember, but it was pretty heated. I think she was leaving him.'

Her words take me by surprise and I try to make sense of them. It's possible, of course; Gabby often kept quiet about things, never telling anyone what she was planning until suddenly she'd make a big announcement that would shock us all. Then I recall that she wanted to tell me something earlier that evening. I never did find out what it was.

'Shaun never said anything,' I say.

'He didn't have to. In the end, after Seffie, she cut us all off, so he saved face by keeping quiet and letting us think she didn't want any of us in her life. But she was leaving Shaun before Seffie went missing. I don't think she even wanted him at that party, but she couldn't not invite him if we were all going.'

I try to make sense of what Anna is telling me – if it's the truth – but even if Gabby *was* leaving Shaun, it's hard to see how that fits in with Seffie. Or what Anna was doing searching through Gabby's things. I urge Anna to continue.

'I chatted to her in her bedroom, then she said she had to go and help her neighbour with something.'

Now I know Anna is lying.

'Gabby got that call in the kitchen,' I say. 'When I was with her. And she went straight out through the back door. There wouldn't have been time to talk to you. Anna, why are you lying?'

'I'm not! Why would I lie? Gabby told me she was going to her neighbour's house and then she left. I was worried about her. I even watched from the window and saw her going across the road.'

'But I heard her talking on the phone. To her neighbour.'

Anna shrugs. 'I don't know what to say. Maybe Gabby was lying? You can ask her when she comes back from wherever she's swanned off to.'

The image of Gabby lying in the garage forces itself into my head, snatching my breath. Anna doesn't seem to notice I'm struggling.

'None of this explains why you were searching through Gabby's things,' I say, trying to keep my voice measured. If Anna is the one who killed Gabby, I can't let her suspect I know the truth.

Anna glances at the door. 'I never told anyone this, because... I was trying to protect Gabby. But... when I saw her walking across the road... Seffie ran after her.'

I'm stunned.

'I couldn't hear what they were saying, but Gabby was shouting at her. Probably telling her to get back in the house. And then...' Anna lowers her head. 'She hit Seffie. Smacked her around the head. And pushed her away.'

'No... Gabby wouldn't do that.' But I remember something. Seffie finding me in the garden office. Telling me something awful had happened. Is this what she was talking about? Not something Andre did? Bile fills my throat.

'It's true,' Anna says. 'I'm sorry. But I've kept Gabby's secret long enough. And that's why I was in her room. I'd seen her writing something in a blue notebook, and when she realised I'd come into the kitchen she quickly closed it. She looked cagey. There's something in that notebook, Sasha. What if Gabby did something to Seffie?'

'But did you see Gabby go into her neighbour's house?'

'Yes.'

'And Seffie came back inside?'

'Yeah. At least, I think so.'

'Then it couldn't have been Gabby.'

'Not then. But what if something happened later?'

My head pounds; I don't know if I can trust Anna. I need to find out if this new information is true. And Gabby can't defend herself. But the police would have checked how long Gabby was at Mrs Fitzpatrick's – so it's unlikely she came back and did anything to Seffie. And what would her motive be? Anna has to be lying. The only thing I can trust is that Anna saw Gabby with a notebook.

'I'm sorry I lied about stealing things,' Anna says. 'You just caught me off-guard and I panicked. But we need to find that notebook. I think there are things in there about Seffie.'

I nod. But there is no way I can let Anna find it.

'You won't tell the others about this, will you? Even Fin. I know you two have got close again, I can see it. The way he looks at you. It's just like it was all those years ago.'

I can't bring myself to be comforted by her words; it doesn't matter what Fin and I have, it can never come to anything. I don't want always to be reminded about poor Seffie.

Before I can answer, Shaun appears, nodding to us as he heads to the coffee machine. 'Any sign of Gabby?' he asks.

Anna and I both shake our heads.

Shaun sighs. 'What the hell? What is she doing?'

My pulse quickens, and guilt swarms inside me. I'm not the one who has killed Gabby, but I know where she is. And that feels almost as bad, as if I'm complicit.

I watch Shaun – he's been the one person I haven't been able to tie to Seffie. As far as I remember, he didn't even speak to her that night. As unreliable as it is, my memory holds no image of Shaun interacting with her. But that doesn't mean he didn't.

My chance to talk to him alone comes when Anna announces she needs to get dressed.

'Shaun,' I begin. 'I know what happened with you and Gabby the first night we got here. I know you slept together.'

He looks up. 'Gabby told you, then. I didn't think she would. She seemed to regret it the next morning. Told me it would never happen again.' He shakes his head. 'Her last words to me were full of hatred.'

I don't admit that I saw them, and that I heard their argument on Christmas Eve. 'I was going to tell Gabby the truth,' I lie. 'About having no memory of that night. And now she's disappeared. It feels... too much of a coincidence.'

He stares at me, his eyes narrowing. 'What are you saying?'

I lower my voice. 'I'm just struggling to understand what she's doing by disappearing.'

'Gabby's got... some issues,' Shaun says. 'She always did, didn't she? She drank to hide them. When we were younger, we probably didn't notice it so much. We were all about partying, weren't we? It was different with Gabby's drinking, but I loved her anyway. She was hard to be with sometimes, but... you can't help who you love, can you?'

I stay silent but I don't agree with Shaun. I believe we can control our feelings if we truly want to. I've done it with Fin for years. I finish my coffee; it's bitter and sticks in my throat. 'I think Gabby holds us all responsible for Seffie,' I say. 'She thinks we all know what happened. She's manipulating us. Has been since she invited us all here. This isn't meant to be a friendly reunion.'

'No,' Shaun says. 'I don't believe that. Gabby wouldn't—'

I feel bad for Shaun, if he's innocent, but I have to continue. 'And how do you know what she would or wouldn't do? You haven't seen her for years. None of us knows each other any more. And we're all here thinking that we do, judging each other on how we were in the past. But that was *twelve years* ago – we were barely adults.'

'Actually,' Shaun says, 'I *have* seen her.'

Heavy silence falls around us.

'What?'

Shaun clears his throat. 'Gabby contacted me a couple of years after Seffie disappeared. And we met up. Then it happened a few more times, until it was at least two or three times a year.'

'Why did she want to?' I ask. 'And why did *you*?'

He clears his throat again. 'Well, I can't speak for Gabby, but for me it was... I don't know. We still had a connection. I still loved her. I know how sad that sounds. It's not like I didn't move on. I met Alia, and she's great. But... I think it's possible to love two people at the same time. In different ways.'

This explains how Gabby and Shaun so quickly slipped into a sexual entanglement on Christmas Eve. It wasn't the first time. 'You should have left her alone,' I say, anger swirling inside me. 'So that Gabby could try to heal. She told us she couldn't see us again, that it was too painful and we'd only be a constant reminder of Seffie. So why would she contact you?'

'That's what I wanted to find out. At first, I thought it was because she loved me, but I was just fooling myself. Gabby didn't love me. At least, not any more. She wanted something else from me.'

'Like what?'

He shrugs. 'I don't know. But she wanted to talk about Seffie all the time. And that night. It was like she was grilling me. And then one day she just cut me off again, until she called to invite us all here.'

I stare at Shaun's arms. He's not excessively muscular, but is nicely toned.

And then it all floods back to me.

Shaun watches me staring at him and frowns. 'Sasha, what is it?'

But I can't speak.

He studies my face. 'I knew this would happen. You know, don't you?'

TWENTY-ONE
BEFORE

Sasha opens her eyes, disorientated. It takes her a second to work out where she is. The garden office. But she has no idea why. It's only when she's aware of how dry her throat feels that she remembers Fin went to get her some water. Suddenly she feels cold, and she sees her dress on the floor. She's naked. Waiting for Fin.

Outside, she hears her name being called, then the door opens. Finally, Fin has come back for her.

'Come here,' she says, smiling. 'I want you now.' Her head swims, but she tries to ignore it. She's waited too long for this.

By the door he hesitates, staring at her. But then he walks over to her. 'Well, this is a surprise,' he says, glancing at her dress on the floor, then taking in every inch of her naked body.

But it isn't, is it? Fin knew this was going to happen. She feels spaced out as he reaches out for her, stroking her breasts, kissing her neck. 'So sexy.' He groans and Sasha closes her eyes. Fin's drunk, but she doesn't care – she's not exactly in control of herself either.

'I'd better lock the door,' he says. 'In case anyone comes in. Seffie's loitering around.'

Seffie. Sasha's sure she was just in here, trying to talk to her. Telling her something had happened, but the fragments of their conversation don't form a cohesive whole.

'Oh, Sasha, you're so beautiful,' Fin says. 'Are you sure you want this? I don't want you to do anything you're not ready for.'

She wants to laugh. She's not a virgin, far from it. But she's never done this with Fin. 'Mmm, Fin,' she says, but her voice sounds weird, like it's not really her.

He pauses for a moment, and she's about to ask him what's wrong, but then he reaches between her legs. He groans again, and she feels him pushing into her. She closes her eyes and dark patterns swirl behind her eyelids. He moans, his soft kisses becoming more urgent. 'Do you like it?' he asks. But she can't answer. She's not even sure if she's moving. Why does she feel so strange?

He slows down and collapses on top of her, running his fingers through her hair. 'That was... amazing.' More kisses. Gentle. First her mouth, then her neck. Then her breasts, and then lower.

And all the while, Sasha can't move. Can't work out why she's not in control of her limbs.

They lie there for a moment, their bodies entwined, and then Fin gets up. 'I'd better go and make sure no one's missing us,' he says.

She hears the zip of his jeans, then his footsteps as he walks away. When he gets to the door, she tells him to wait, but she can barely lift her head, and can't even see him any more.

'You forgot my water,' she says.

Shaun shrugs. 'Okay, I'll get you some water.'

TWENTY-TWO

NOW

08:15

Sasha stares at Shaun as flashes of memory flood back to her. 'What did you do to me?' she cries, nausea threatening to explode like a bomb in her body. 'The night of the party. What did you do?' Hot tears sting her cheeks.

'Shh, lower your voice.' Shaun looks around. 'I didn't do anything to you,' he hisses. 'You... you said you wanted me. I was looking for Gabby, and there you were on the sofa. In that garden office. Naked. You told me you wanted me.'

For the second time in a few hours, Sasha vomits. It trickles down the side of the table, pooling on the floor, but she can't move to clean it up. She swipes at her mouth. 'No... no... I was waiting for Fin. He was coming back with my water. We'd been waiting to... Oh, Jesus. I thought you were Fin.'

'That's bullshit,' Shaun says. 'You're saying that because you regretted it after. You basically cheated on Fin, the great love of your life. And there you've been, making snide comments to me about having a wife at home while I'm here with Gabby. You're a hypocrite, Sasha.'

I stare at him, unable to grasp what I'm hearing. His words are from a nightmare I need to wake up from. 'Why would you think I'd sleep with you? You were Gabby's boyfriend. Fin's best friend. *My* friend.'

His face softens. 'We were all drunk, Sasha. Things happen. The six of us were so close, weren't we? It's easy to get caught up in things when you spend so much time with people. I'm sorry if you think I took advantage of you. I was so out of it.'

'Not too out of it to have sex!'

Shaun ignores me. 'Gabby and I had argued. An awful one. Said things neither of us could take back. I accused her of cheating on me. I was so sure she was. I could just feel it. I wasn't in a good place.'

'Don't you dare make excuses!' I scream.

'Please, be quiet! Do you want everyone to know what happened? How does it make us look? And Fin... Jesus, he'd kill me! I've never seen someone so besotted. That man still loves you after all this time. If he found out, then—'

I ram my fist into Shaun's face. Over and over until he grabs my wrists. 'Enough!'

'Why the fuck would you do that? To me! To Fin. You knew I was drunk!' *But it was more than that. Alcohol alone wouldn't have done that to me.* 'Did you drug me? Put something in my drink?'

'No! I would never—'

'I'm calling the police. You... you *raped* me!'

'Jesus Christ, no I *didn't*! You were there naked on the sofa, telling me you wanted me. That's not rape, Sasha!'

'I thought you were Fin! I would never have slept with you.'

'Well, I hate to break it to you, but you did.'

'What will your wife say when she finds out? And she should know about you sleeping with Gabby the other night.'

Shaun's eyes widen. 'I've got two kids, Sasha. Don't destroy my life.'

'Like you have mine?'

'You didn't even remember it until just now, did you? I could see it on your face.'

But there was always something about Shaun lurking in the depths of my mind. I thought it was about Seffie, but now I know it was always about me and Shaun. Seeing him with Gabby the other night must have triggered something.

I feel sickened, violated. As if I'm not the person I thought I was. Again. 'The truth always comes out, Shaun. The truth about everything.'

'Don't fuck with me, Sasha.'

Leaving my cup on the table, I stand, ready to leave, but Shaun grabs my arm, gripping my wrist so tightly I gasp. 'If you tell the police, or anyone else, my life will be over. So I might have to take stupid risks, Sasha. Do things I wouldn't usually ever consider. You know, to protect my family.'

I yank my arm from his grip and leave the room, with Shaun's threat ringing loudly in my ears.

10:30

'I've been waiting to talk to you all morning,' Fin says, when I find him in his room. 'I managed to get hold of the police. They'll come as soon as they can.' He reaches for my hand. 'Everything will be okay.'

I take a deep breath. 'Thank God.'

'We just have to get through this until they get here. Okay?'

I nod.

'How are you doing? I'm guessing you didn't get any sleep last night. I know I didn't.'

'Not really.' I sit on the bed, gathering my thoughts. I want to tell Fin about Shaun, but I have no evidence that I was drugged. Or that, if I was, he was the one who did it. Shaun could make out that I've concocted this story because I regretted sleeping with him. But even if I keep his heinous secret, I will make sure that he takes responsibility for what he did.

And if he could do that to me, then what else is he capable of?

I think of the video cameras, which will have recorded Shaun and I talking in the kitchen. But without sound, there's no evidence of what happened back then in the garden office. And now that I've had a couple of hours to reflect, I doubt there's any way I could prove I didn't know it was Shaun. But he knows the truth. I called Fin's name, I know I did.

'Sasha? You okay?'

Fin's voice brings me back to the present. 'Anna wants to leave,' I say. 'And she seems to think Gabby might have had something to do with Seffie disappearing.' I explain what Anna told me about witnessing Gabby hitting Seffie when she'd followed her to Mrs Fitzpatrick's. 'I think that's what Seffie wanted to tell me when she said something awful had happened. But I can't remember. And to be honest, I don't even know if that was real, or if my mind conjured it up somehow.'

Fin considers this. 'But I suppose that doesn't mean Gabby did anything to Seffie. And you said Anna saw her come back safe after that.'

'But what if Seffie ran away because of what Gabby did? And then something happened to her? It might not even have been any of us. A stranger could have...' I can't bring myself to finish this thought.

'I'm not even sure that matters any more,' Fin says. 'Gabby is dead, and she didn't do it to herself.'

I need to find that notebook. Someone in this house has it. Gabby's murderer. I'm about to tell Fin about it but he takes my arm.

'Sash, I need to tell you something. I got a call this morning from Ravinder, just after I managed to get hold of the police. She's been trying to get hold of me. She had some bad news. A few days ago, she went to hospital for some tests. She'd been having abnormal bleeding and was just ignoring it. I told her she needed to get it checked out. Practically forced her to go. Anyway, she told me they called her with the results on the day I left to come here. She's got endometrial cancer. It doesn't look good. Stage four.'

I wrap my arms around him. 'Oh, Fin, I'm sorry.'

'Yeah, thanks.' He pulls back, dabbing his eyes. 'She said she didn't want to tell me as I was coming up here. She wanted me to enjoy Christmas with my friends. Can you believe she put my happiness before anything else? That's the kind of woman she is. When we get out of here, I'm going to go back to support her through this. She doesn't have any family. They all live in America and she's refusing to tell them until after the new year.' Fin's eyes well with tears. 'But who knows how much longer she'll have.'

'She's lucky to have you in her life,' I say, feeling tears prick my own eyes.

'Before I left to come up here, I told her about you.'

'Oh! That must have been hard.'

'But do you know what she said? She told me I had to fight for you. That when something is that strong, you have to hold onto it and never let it go.'

I hold him tightly, tears falling fast now because I can't give Fin what he wants.

'Come back with me,' he says. 'When we can leave. We can give it a go and I can still be around to support Ravinder. You'd like her, I know you would, and she'd love you.'

In this moment, I know what I have to do.

'I never loved you,' I say, the tears I force back stinging my eyes. 'I'm sorry. But it was never real. We were too young to know what love is.' I walk over to the window, stare out at the loch. I can't look at Fin while I say this, because he'll surely see through my lies. No one knows me like he does. 'If I met you now, I'd never want to be with you.'

'Don't say that. You don't mean that, Sash.'

'Yes, I do. I know we're stuck here for now, but I want you to stay away from me and leave me alone. We would never have lasted. It's a fantasy to think that we could have.'

Fin stares at me, his face crumpling. I've destroyed him, and the memory of us he's held so close to his heart. But this is the best way. It's the only way.

Eventually, he stands, wiping his eyes. 'You've clearly made your mind up.'

'Just go, Fin.'

I desperately want to give him a hug, but instead I push him through the door, closing it before he sees my stream of tears.

And then I sink to the floor.

I'm truly alone in this now, and fear grips hold of me, crushing me until it feels like I can't breathe.

TWENTY-THREE

NOW

14:45

I stay in my room, staring out at the loch, and the rugged snow-covered mountains beyond. It feels like I'm looking at a picture and living in a nightmare. Because of Shaun, everything that ever existed between Fin and me has been sullied. If I could go back to that first day at university, I would have sat on the other side of the lecture hall, far away from Gabby. That's how it all started with the six of us. Gabby already knew Shaun, and through him we met Fin and Andre. Anna came a few weeks later. She'd got a last-minute place and had missed the beginning of term, but she strolled into our seminar with such confidence that Gabby and I couldn't help being drawn to her.

And now, if I could erase it all, I would. Each and every one of them.

When I venture out of my room in the afternoon, I pass Andre on the stairs. 'Are you okay?' he asks. 'Fin's in his room, if you're looking for him.'

'I'm not,' I say, too harshly.

'Oh,' Andre says. 'Are you okay? Has something happened?' He studies my tear-stained cheeks.

'It's none of your business,' I snap.

Andre's face falls. 'Sorry, I didn't mean—'

'All of us are leaving as soon as we can,' I say. 'We'll never have to see each other again. So why don't you just tell me truth about those messages? I know they're from you. I've kept them. Every single one of them. All the evidence of your stalking and harassment I need to go to the police with.' I pull my phone from my pocket, begin scrolling. I could select any one of the hundreds of messages, the meaning in each one is clear. 'Here,' I say. *'We'll always be tied together because of what happened, won't we? I take comfort in that. An unbreakable bond.* Oh, and here's another. *You were meant to come into my life. All of you. But especially you.'*

'Sasha, please, just stop.'

'No, Andre. You didn't stop, did you? Even when I replied, telling you to leave me alone. The messages just ramped up after that. You need help.'

'I probably do,' he says. 'But I'm getting sick of telling you I did not send you any messages. I moved on with my life, Sasha. I admit it took a while, but I threw myself into my master's degree and then found a great job. I was happy. I even met someone. Cleo. We were together for eight years.'

I stare at him, searching his face for signs of dishonesty, but I can't find any. He's just Andre. The same person he always was. Quiet and honest. 'I... I had no idea you were with someone. You never said.'

'Nobody ever asked. Everyone probably just assumed I've been on my own since uni. Just because I'm quiet and keep to myself. I'm a private person, Sasha, just like I always was.'

Andre's right. All of us had overlooked him because he was so good at blending into the background. Listening to us instead of talking about himself. As if what was happening with him didn't matter.

But he lied about being alone with Seffie in her room, so I still can't trust him. Maybe he didn't send me those messages, but that doesn't mean he's innocent. 'Have you heard from Gabby?' I ask.

There's a flicker of hesitation, I'm sure of it. 'No. This was all probably just too much for her. Anna noticed her bag, coat and phone are gone.'

After finding Gabby's body, I hadn't even considered searching for her phone. Things she might take with her if she was leaving the house. Clearly, her killer has thought of everything.

'What's wrong?' Andre says. 'Are you ill?'

I brush past him. 'I need some water.'

19:08

The four of us sit at Gabby's large dining table, eating Anna's home-made pizzas and salad. 'Sorry they're a bit crispy,' she says. But I doubt any of us has noticed. The others went out searching for Gabby again before we sat down to eat, but I couldn't keep up the pretence so I stayed here. And Fin hasn't come down from his room, telling Shaun he has a migraine.

Throughout the meal, I feel eyes are on me. Anna with her desperation to find Gabby's notebook. Shaun, knowing what he did to me that night. And Andre, who I can't read but now I don't trust. Everyone sitting at this table, including me, is a liar.

'I didn't think there could be a worse Christmas than 2012,' Shaun says, steepling his hands together and glancing at me. 'But this is bloody close.'

'How can you say that?' Anna says, shoving her plate aside. She's barely touched a thing, even though it was her idea to make pizza. 'Seffie disappeared. What could be worse than that?'

'How about Gabby disappearing?' I say, my words filled with indignation.

No one speaks. Each of us must know by now that what happened at Christmas twelve years ago is happening all over again.

'I can't wait until we can get the fuck out of here,' Shaun says. 'This has been a complete shitshow.' He glares at me, and I wonder if anyone else notices he's singling me out.

He has no idea the police are on their way, and that they'll get here before any of us can leave. 'The truth always comes out,' I say, pushing my plate aside.

Shaun's eyebrows knit together. 'I don't think it does. People get away with things all the time.'

As I sit here, I realise there's only one way I will get through the long wait for the police, and that's if I know who I have to fear. This is the only way I can hope to protect myself. 'As soon as I get home, I'm going straight to the police. I'm telling them everything,' I announce. 'I know I didn't harm Seffie in any way, but someone who was at Gabby's party that Christmas Eve did. The police can reopen the investigation, with all the facts this time. Everything.' I smile at Shaun. 'And memory is the funniest thing. It's always still there, lurking. Waiting to be triggered.'

I've done it now, and there's no going back. I am the bait that will make Gabby's murderer reveal themselves. This is the way I will find Gabby's notebook.

Silence hangs over us, broken only when Anna pushes her chair back and stands. 'Well, I don't care what you do,' she says. 'As soon as we can get out of here, I'm heading straight to the airport. And I'm not coming back. There's nothing for me in the UK any more. That's patently clear.' She flicks her hair back over her shoulder.

'Do what you have to do, Sasha,' Andre says. 'I've got nothing to hide.'

Only that you were alone with Seffie in her room. Did Gabby find out? Is that why she's lying dead on the garage floor?

Shaun is the last to speak. 'You're crazy,' he says. 'Am I the only one who can see that? This is insane! We don't need to involve the police.'

'If you've got nothing to hide then there's nothing to worry about,' I say.

01:32

For a couple of hours, I manage to fight sleep, forcing myself to read things on my phone, looking through old photos, praying that the glare of the screen will keep me alert. I listen out for noises, hoping to hear something – anything – because the silence is terrifying.

At some point, I drift off, and when my eyes shoot open, there's someone in my room, standing by the door. My eyes squint to see in the darkness.

'Shaun,' I say, pulling myself up. I shouldn't be surprised that he's the one who's come to me.

He steps forward and walks to the end of my bed. 'You can't go to the police, Sasha.'

A heavy lump lodges in my throat. I hadn't bargained on how vulnerable I would feel – even though under the duvet I'm fully dressed, and in my hand I hold Gabby's largest kitchen knife.

'I've got young kids. Shall I tell you about them? You've never even asked.' He steps forward again. 'They're called Tilly and Freddie. They're twins. Four years old. Did you know we had to have IVF? That we went through hell to have them? No, course you didn't. Just because I laugh and make jokes doesn't mean I haven't suffered in my life.' He walks closer to me. 'And they're the sweetest kids.' He smiles. 'Not always, oh yeah, they have their moments. Drive Alia and me crazy sometimes. But they're... they're *innocent*.' He sits on the bed. 'They've never done anything wrong. They shouldn't have to pay for *my* mistakes.'

'But *you* have to. You know that, don't you?'

He shakes his head. 'No, Sasha, I can't let that happen.'

TWENTY-FOUR
BEFORE

Anna sits alone in the kitchen, pouring herself another glass. She's never felt so rejected, and it sickens her. Even off his face, Shaun didn't go for it when she handed herself to him on a plate. Perhaps she's been wrong about him, and he really does love Gabby. She struggles to believe that, though. People don't change who they fundamentally are. The essence of us is fixed. But what gets to her most is the look of disgust she saw on his face. That's what's eating her up. She's only ever seen people look at her with lust in their eyes, not horror. And she doesn't know how to deal with it.

She pours more alcohol down her throat, and her thoughts turn to Gabby. She still hasn't come back from her neighbour's house and Anna's starting to worry. When she spoke to Gabby in her room earlier, she'd seemed fine, a bit drunk maybe, but nothing else. And the pill Anna slipped into her drink should have worked by now. Just a little something to loosen Gabby up, because Anna doesn't believe for one second that it's over between them. And maybe, if it was going to be over between them, she wanted one last time to relish. She can't understand how she's fallen so hard for Gabby, when it's just not like her to get attached to anyone. But they've grown close over the years, and Gabby has got under her skin. And unlike Shaun, Anna *sees* her. Understands her. She just wishes Gabby would realise that Shaun is not the person she's meant to be with.

Now, Anna's slowly beginning to realise that trying to seduce Shaun to make Gabby jealous was a low move. Juvenile and pathetic. Desperate and needy. And that just makes her feel worse about herself, because it's not her. It's as if she's been stripped of her power.

She thinks of her parents, and that always-present feeling of not being enough. Clever enough. Pretty enough. Just *enough*. And now Shaun has turned her into that girl again, the one she swore she'd never again let herself be.

The back door opens and Fin comes in. 'Hey,' he says.

Anna lifts her hand to wave, because speaking is far too much effort.

'I've just come to get Sasha some water. Her head's not right. She seems really spaced out, and she's hardly drunk anything.'

'Oh,' Anna says, biting her lip. She'd given drinks to Gabby and Sasha earlier. What if she'd got them mixed up? It would explain why Gabby didn't seem to be affected by the pill. Anna dismisses this thought. She was too careful. That can't be what's happened. Gabby, a hardened drinker, might just have a body that can tolerate anything.

She watches Fin filling a glass with water, and marvels at how much he dotes on Sasha, even though they're technically not even together. Yet. She's sure that will change tonight, now that they're both finally single.

She doesn't even notice that she's crying until Fin rushes over to her, leaving Sasha's water by the sink. 'Anna, what is it? Are you okay?' Large tears fall into her glass.

Mortified that she's lost control of herself, she shakes her head. And then all she knows is that she has to get out of this kitchen before she suffocates. Jumping up, she bolts for the door and rushes into the garden, around the side of the house where she knows there's a gate leading to the front. She will just run from them all and never look back.

'Anna, wait!'

She hears Fin's voice but she ignores him, almost reaching the gate before Fin catches up with her. 'Hey, stop. Talk to me. What's going on?'

His voice is so kind, so gentle, and it only makes her feel worse. She doesn't deserve his concern. He's a good man. Sasha is lucky.

Fin grabs her arm to stop her reaching the gate. 'Please talk to me. Let me help.'

Anna sinks to the concrete, not caring how cold it is against her bare legs. Physical pain is good, she needs it to numb her emotional anguish. Fin sits beside her, holding her arm. 'I'm not a good person,' she says.

'Course you are. Why are you saying this? What's happened, Anna?'

She should tell him about Shaun, how she tried to sleep with him just to get back at Gabby. To prove a point. And how she's been sleeping with Gabby too, even though she's fully aware that Gabby wasn't entirely sure about what she was doing. Anna should have left her alone. Both of them. But now she's played with fire and everything's a hideous mess.

'*I* happened,' she says. 'I don't deserve any of you.'

Her hair, damp from her tears, sticks to her face, and Fin moves it from her cheek. She grabs his arm and pulls him close to her, leaning into him and kissing his neck, desperate to feel close to someone. Desperate to be wanted.

'Anna, I don't think—'

'Please, Fin. I need this. I need you.'

He hesitates, but there's something there, she can sense it. 'I'm drunk,' he says.

But when she strokes his leg, and moves her hand higher, he doesn't protest.

And then she's kissing his soft mouth, expecting any second that he'll push her away, and she'll see that same look of disgust she saw on Shaun's face earlier. She can't let that happen. Pushing him back, she unzips his jeans and climbs on top of him, pulling her dress over her head so he can see all of her. She just wants him to look at her and desire her.

'Anna, I can't,' he protests, but he's already inside her and his body is enjoying it too much to stop.

Anna feels wanted again; this is all she's needed. She pushes down further, relishing his ecstatic groan, and then when she looks up, Seffie is standing there watching them.

'Jesus!' Anna scrambles up and grabs her dress, covering herself as much as she can. 'What are you doing, Seffie?'

It takes Fin a second to work out what's going on, and when he does, in the light of the full moon, she can see how stricken his face is. How terrified.

'I'm telling Sasha!' Seffie screams, and then she's running, towards the garden office. She pounds on the door, calling for Sasha.

Anna rushes after her, yelling for her to stop, but it's Fin who catches up with her first, taking her arm and coaxing her away from the office. 'Please, Seffie, that wasn't what it looked like. I love Sasha! Anna and I... we weren't doing anything. Please, can we just talk to you and explain?'

Fin is not doing a good job of convincing Seffie. Anna should handle this.

But Seffie, tears streaming down her face, turns and runs. Anna tries to grab her, but she pulls away, darting towards the woods.

And then Anna loses sight of her.

TWENTY-FIVE

NOW

01:34

'I can't let you destroy my life,' Shaun repeats.

I pull the duvet off and get out of bed, holding the knife behind my back. 'There's nothing you can do. However much you try to threaten me.' As terrified as I am, I somehow manage to keep my voice calm. But my shaking hands betray me. Unknown to Shaun, the cameras are filming this – proof that I've attacked him in self-defence.

'Threaten you? I'm not threatening you, Sasha.' He moves towards me.

And now I wish I hadn't pushed Fin away. 'Everything comes back to haunt us, Shaun. All these lies we tell. It eats away at us. It's time for it to end. We all need to face up to whatever we've done.'

'I haven't done *anything*,' he says. 'You wanted to sleep with me. You told me those exact words. *I want you*. That's what you said to me. You were naked. I can still picture you clearly now.'

For a second, I feel a flicker of doubt. But there's no way. 'Stop! You drugged me! If it seemed like I wanted you, it's because of what you put in my drink!' It sickens me to have this conversation again with him. Being around him at all is too much. 'I thought you were Fin.'

'Keep telling yourself that.'

'How could you have thought I enjoyed it? I could barely move.'

Shaun doesn't say anything, but I know I've offended him.

'What you did to me pales in comparison to the other stuff you've done,' I say.

He screws up his face. 'What other stuff? What the hell are you talking about?' He steps closer to me and I catch his scent, activating memories that I wish had stayed buried.

There's a sound outside the door. A flash of light in the hall. Anna pokes her head around the door, shining her phone's torch into the room. She glances between Shaun and me, frowning. 'I thought I heard voices. What's going on?'

'Nothing,' Shaun says, backing away from me.

'It doesn't look like nothing. What is this?'

'Just leave it, Anna!' Shaun barks, storming out of the room.

'What was all that about?' Anna whispers, shutting the door after him.

'He doesn't want the truth to come out,' I say. And in part, this is true. Relief floods through my body; Anna has unwittingly prevented Shaun doing anything to me, and I'm silently grateful for that. 'How come you're up?'

'I can't sleep,' she says. 'I need to find Gabby's notebook. I've been looking again, while everyone's asleep. Or at least, I thought they were.'

'There's every chance she's taken it with her.'

Anna sits on the bed cross-legged and rests her head in her hands. 'Maybe. But the tiny handbag she had by the door is missing, and that wouldn't have fitted the notebook in.'

Or is there another reason Anna is so sure it's here?

'I just think we need to find it,' she continues, looking up and staring at the ceiling. 'Are you sure you haven't seen it?'

'Yes, I'm sure.'

Her eyes narrow. 'Well, let's keep looking. It's not like we've got anywhere else to be.' She leans forward and gives me a hug. 'Goodnight, Sasha.'

As soon as the door closes, I realise there's one place I hadn't even thought of looking. Immediately, I check in all the drawers in my room, but they're empty except for spare towels and bedding. I lift up the towels, and there underneath them is an envelope. Glancing at my door, I pull out the envelope and see Gabby's name on it in handwriting I recognise.

With a heavy pain in my chest, I sit on the bed and pull out the paper inside. It's a letter to Gabby, written on the A4 paper we used to use for our university notes.

I start reading, hearing Anna's voice in my head narrating the words. And by the time I've finished, I know all about what had been happening between her and Gabby. I clamp my hand over my mouth. I had no idea. Gabby was supposed to be with Shaun. What surprises me most of all, though, is how attached Anna was to Gabby, her words in this letter begging Gabby to give their relationship a chance. That's the thing that doesn't make sense. Anna doesn't do feelings. She takes what she wants from people and then discards them, even if she tries to do it in a kind way. Why was it different with Gabby?

There's no date on the letter, and having no address or stamp on the envelope must mean that Anna gave it to Gabby before she left for Spain. But it mentions Seffie's disappearance, so Anna wrote it sometime after the party.

I cast my mind back to earlier on the evening Seffie disappeared, remembering that Gabby wanted to talk to me. And she'd been off with Shaun. They'd argued. But according to this letter, she was ending things with Anna, so why would she be off with Shaun? Did he somehow find out about Anna? Is that why he did what he did to me in the garden office? Out of anger, or because he was feeling rejected?

I reread the letter. There's nothing in it that sheds any light on what happened to Seffie – all it does is throw up more questions. And prove that Gabby, too, was as much a liar as the rest of us.

But she had her reasons, and for Gabby to keep quiet, clearly what happened between her and Anna tormented her. But Gabby must have deliberately left the letter here in the room I'm staying in – it didn't get there by accident. The only thing I can't answer is why.

I slip the letter back underneath the towels and climb into bed, no closer to the truth. And still the threat of Shaun coming back hovers over me.

My eyes are just starting to close when my phone pings with a text.

Shocked that a message has actually got through, I freeze when I see the name appear on my phone.

Gabby.

I open WhatsApp and read her message.

Please come. I need help. I'm in the garage.

TWENTY-SIX
BEFORE

Seffie pulls the duvet over her head and closes her eyes. Everyone keeps telling her to go to sleep, but how can she when the music is thumping through the floorboards? Besides, why should Gabby have all the fun with her friends while she's up here alone in her room? Alone, like she always is.

Sometimes Seffie envies her sister. Gabby is so grown up, so beautiful, and she has her friends, who all love her. They're always together, and Seffie can only imagine what it feels like to have proper friends. Actually, she can't even imagine it. She does have Penny at school, kind of. But most of the time Penny wants to play with other people, so Seffie just sits quietly in the playground reading. Everyone thinks she's weird, she knows that, with her head constantly stuck in a book. But the truth is, she's only reading because no one will play with her. She'd much rather be running around, playing the games the other girls in her class won't let her be part of.

That's why Gabby is so lucky, and she doesn't even know it. Her friends are special. They always make time to talk to Seffie, and never make her feel like she's an annoying pain in the butt, which is what Gabby always does.

Seffie recalls the words her sister said to her a few moments ago, when Seffie had seen her going across the road and gone after her.

'Why are you following me? Go to bloody bed, Seffie. Stop ruining this party for me. You always do this. You're always in the bloody way. Creeping about. Spying. It's weird, you know. *You're* weird!'

Gabby's words had struck Seffie like a punch to her stomach. Yes, Gabby has called her annoying before, many times, but she's never said stuff like this. Stuff that the kids at school say to her.

'But—'

'But what? Just leave me alone, will you?' Gabby had pushed her away then – another thing she's never done before. What was wrong with her tonight? Gabby had turned around and rushed down Mrs Fitzgerald's path, letting herself in with the spare key they had. Leaving Seffie in the middle of the street on her own.

Now, Seffie gets out of bed and stands in front of the mirror, inspecting herself. *One day I'll be beautiful like Gabby. And popular*. Smiling, she changes into the silver dress she loves so much but has never had a chance to wear. And then she sneaks downstairs again.

Hearing 'All I Want For Christmas' makes her want to dance, so she does, even though Andre is in the living room. He gives her that look, the one that says she shouldn't be down here, but he doesn't have a go at her, just asks her what she's doing. She convinces Andre to let her stay until the song's finished, then he takes her upstairs. Gabby would never do that – she'd just bark the order for Seffie to go up, she wouldn't take the time to go with her.

At the top of the stairs, Seffie tells Andre she's scared being alone in her room with the door shut. She isn't, but if it keeps him talking to her for longer then she'll say anything. It works, and he agrees to come in and check her room for her. Make sure there's nothing scary in there. As if! She's not five.

Grabbing Mr Cuddles from the foot of her bed, Seffie sits and tries to keep Andre talking. It's nice to have company. She asks him if he likes Gabby, just for something to say.

'No, I'm not interested in your sister.'

'Hmm. All men are.' Women too. She's seen Gabby and Anna kissing, but keeps that information to herself. It might come in handy one day. 'Come on,' she says. 'You must like Gabby. I'm not going to sleep until you tell me.'

Andre leans forward and whispers, 'Want me to tell you a secret, Seraphina?'

Excited, Seffie nods. 'Yes.'

'There is someone I like. She's beautiful. And kind. She's really special, actually. Nobody knows. I... I can't tell anyone. It just... wouldn't be good.'

Seffie giggles. She likes gossip. Especially if it's something Gabby doesn't know.

'Who is it?' she asks.

Andre hesitates, getting up to look out of the window. 'Can I trust you?'

She nods again.

'It's Sasha. I'm in love with her, but I can never let her know. She loves Fin. There's no space for me.'

Seffie feels sad. 'I'm sorry. I like Sasha. But she really loves Fin. They're supposed to be together. Everyone knows it.'

Andre sighs. 'I know. That's why I'll never say anything to her. But also because I know that even if she wasn't with Fin, she wouldn't be with me.'

Seffie frowns. 'Why not? She might like you if Fin wasn't with her.'

Andre blushes. 'No, she doesn't. When you're an adult, you'll realise. Some people are just never meant to be with us, even if we have strong feelings for them. You can sense when there's a connection. And we can't have a connection with everyone.'

Seffie's not entirely sure what he's talking about, but she leans forward and gives him a hug, because that's what it feels like he needs.

'Hey, what's that for?' Andre asks.

'Just because you're nice.'

'Well, thanks. But I think it's time you got to bed now, don't you?'

'No,' she says.

'Come on, Seraphina. I need to get back downstairs. Everyone will be wondering where I am.'

She springs up and rushes to the door, but Andre's too quick and he reaches his arm out to stop her. 'Ow!' Seffie cries, clutching her cheek. She must have caught it on Andre's watch.

'Oh, God, I'm so sorry. Are you okay?' Andre leans forward to examine her face. 'I didn't mean to... I'm so sorry, Seraphina.'

'It's okay,' she says. 'It was an accident.' And if she's honest with herself, it was her fault for trying to run downstairs. He was only being kind to her, and she took advantage of him. 'I'll go and clean it up in the bathroom,' she says. 'And then I promise I'll go to bed.'

'Okay,' Andre says.

He looks so worried and Seffie feels sorry for him. She really needs to keep her promise.

Try as she might, Seffie still can't settle to sleep. The music pounds, and she's not even sure if Gabby's back. She wants to say sorry to her sister for annoying her so much. And she's thirsty. Hungry, too. A nice crunchy apple would help fill her stomach.

Opening her door a crack, she checks to make sure the hallway is empty. People keep using the bathroom up here and they shouldn't be when there's a perfectly good toilet downstairs. When she's sure the coast is clear, she makes her way to the kitchen.

She slips past the living room, where she can hear Andre and Shaun talking about football. Anna and Fin are in the kitchen, and Seffie's about to stroll in and announce that she's just here for water and an apple, but then she notices Anna is crying. It's strange – she's never seen Anna upset before. Intrigued, Seffie steps closer to the door. They still haven't noticed she's there. Not surprising, when she's invisible to most people. Fin rushes over to Anna, asking her what's wrong, but Anna ignores him and jumps up, throwing the back door open and rushing outside.

When Fin goes after Anna, Seffie follows.

She's freezing outside in just her pyjamas, but she doesn't care. She wants to know what's going on. Anna and Fin disappear around the side of the house and, silently, Seffie follows, keeping to the edge of the garden by the trees so there might be less chance she'll be seen. Gabby will kill her if she knows Seffie's been spying on her friends. And she doesn't want to be called weird again.

She watches Anna sink to the floor, and Fin does the same. She's talking about how she doesn't deserve any of them. Then she is kissing him, and Seffie feels sick. Fin is Sasha's boyfriend, not Anna's. What are they doing?

And it only gets worse. Stunned, Seffie is unable to move when Anna pulls her dress over her head and she and Fin do things Seffie's heard adults do, but that make her want to throw up. And all she can think is that she has to tell Sasha.

Before she can move, Anna is looking straight at her with wide, wild eyes. 'Jesus!' she says, scrambling for her dress. 'What are you doing, Seffie?'

'I'm telling Sasha!' Seffie screams. She runs towards the garden office. All she knows is that she has to find Sasha.

But Sasha doesn't respond when Seffie pounds on the door. 'Sasha! Let me in! Something awful's happened!' Nothing. No answer. Maybe she's not even in there. Fin grabs her arm, leading her away from the door, telling her that he can explain.

Seffie runs, managing to avoid Anna, who reaches out to grab her. They're scaring her. Anna looks so angry. And the only place Seffie can go to get away is into the woods.

TWENTY-SEVEN

NOW

02:17

Feeling sick to my stomach, I rush to Gabby's bedroom and check the cameras, playing back the last few minutes. But everyone is asleep. None of them could have sent me that message. It doesn't make sense. Gabby is dead. I saw her. I checked her pulse. She was dead.

Clutching the kitchen knife, I head downstairs and slip on my boots, unlocking the back door. The garage door is unlocked, just as Fin and I left it last night. With a sickening sense of déjà vu, I step inside and flick the light switch, illuminating the garage.

I walk over to the corner, but Gabby's body isn't there, or the blanket that was covering her. I glance around, but other than the shelves of tools along the back, packing boxes and the mountain bike, the garage is empty.

'Gabby?' I call.

I stare at my phone, reading the message again. *Please come. I need help. I'm in the garage.* And I can't reply to it because once again I have no signal.

Before I can decide what to do, the garage door opens and someone steps out of the shadows.

Fin.

I stare at him, struggling to place him here. It doesn't make sense. And he doesn't look himself. He's not smiling, or rushing over, there's no shock on his face that Gabby's body isn't here.

With sickening clarity, I realise what he's doing here. I hold up the knife. 'What have you done?' I say, edging away from him. 'You...'

He steps inside and closes the door. 'I had to,' he says. 'When I read this.' Keeping his eye on me, he walks over to one of the boxes and pulls out a blue hardback notebook. 'Please, Sasha, you have to believe me. I didn't plan for any of this. This isn't what I wanted. I'm not a... a murderer.' He moves forward, still clutching the notebook. 'Sometimes... sometimes things just happen that are out of our control.'

I grip the knife tightly, backing away from him. I'll use it if I have to, even on Fin. I'll do whatever it takes to protect myself and make him account for what he's done. 'What's in Gabby's notebook?' Even as I say this, I'm unable to comprehend how it's possible that Fin is standing here, telling me this. My Fin.

'I guessed you'd know about this. You and Gabby were always tight, weren't you? Told each other everything. I was hoping that would have changed over the years. I never wanted you to get involved in this.'

Fin's words chill my spine. 'What's in that notebook?'

'I found it in her study when we first got here. I didn't trust her from the second I arrived. It makes for interesting reading. She thought you did something to Seffie.'

'What?' I'm seconds away from throwing up.

'That's what it said. I couldn't let her think it was you, could I?'

So Gabby had been lying to me, trying to get me onside

when I was the one she didn't trust. I back away from him, hold up the knife. 'Why would she think it was me?'

'According to her very detailed notes, it said she'd met up with Shaun a few months ago and they went out for drinks. He was so off his face that he accidentally let something slip about you not remembering everything. That must have made her highly suspicious.'

Fin doesn't know that I admitted this to Gabby in the end.

'So, don't you see? I did this for you. I couldn't let Gabby think you'd harmed Seffie.'

'Don't you dare!' I scream. 'What did you do to Gabby?' I edge back, because even though this is Fin, he's not going to let me get out of here now. Not when he's already killed Gabby.

'Don't worry, I told her the truth about you. She didn't die thinking it was you. That's how much I love you, Sasha. In the end, she knew the truth.'

Tears flood down my cheeks, but still I grip the knife. 'You didn't have to do anything to Gabby! I could have explained it all to her.'

'She caught me with her notebook. And then she wouldn't let it go when I tried to explain I'd just found it. She just kept on and on and on. It was doing my head in.'

I can no longer keep back the contents of my stomach.

Fin rushes towards me. 'Sasha, are you okay?'

I stab the knife towards him. 'Get away from me. Stay back!'

He stops. 'No need for that.'

'You were lying about calling the police. They're not on their way, are they?'

He edges forward again. 'Don't you see that I had to tell you that? To buy myself time to think. You would have called them yourself if I hadn't told you I'd already done it.' He clutches his head. 'This is all such a mess.'

'Everything you've said is a lie, isn't it.'

'No, please don't say that. I love you. That's never been a lie.'

All the things Fin has said since we got to this house play out in my mind. 'Ravinder doesn't have cancer, does she?'

He hangs his head. 'No.'

'Why the hell would you tell me that?'

'Because you were slipping away from me. I needed you to see the good in me again, to realise that I'm a decent man who's worthy of you.'

I shake my head. 'But you're not! You're sick in the head. Deluded. And you sent that message from Gabby's phone.'

'Sorry, I had to. I realise it probably freaked you out. Or got your hopes up. But I had to get you alone. I need you to help me. We can cover this up so the others never find out. Please, Sasha. Someone emailed Gabby to tell her it was one of us. Someone knows about Seffie. We need to stick together, then we can find out who it is and stop them going to the police. I'm sure it's Anna. We need to be careful of her.'

'I will never help you. What the fuck did you do?' I scream. 'Tell me!'

Fin's eyes widen. In his deluded state, he actually expected me to help him. 'You should have left it alone,' he says. His calmness is menacing. 'I'm trying, Sash, I really am. Please listen to me. I never wanted this to happen.'

As I stare at him, I realise that he means it. And somehow that terrifies me even more. It only demonstrates how unhinged he is. 'What did you do to Seffie?' I ask. All these years, I've held onto the hope that one day she'll turn up, but Fin has extinguished that flame I tried so desperately to keep burning. I've edged all the way back to the wall now, and there's nowhere for me to run.

'I loved you, Sasha,' Fin says. 'And I've never stopped. Even when you backed off, and said there was no chance for us after

Seffie, I could never let you go. Our connection can't be severed. Even if you never replied to me.'

With horror, I realise that Fin's talking about the messages I've been getting all these years. I thought it had been Andre stalking me, but he was telling the truth when he insisted it wasn't him. 'All those messages were from you? Why?' I ask, even though I'm sure I already know. 'Why send them anonymously?'

'Because you're mine, Sasha. You always have been, don't you see that? And if you knew they were from me, you wouldn't ever trust me.'

I shake my head. 'No... you're sick, Fin. And the worst thing is, you actually know it. You need help.'

A flash of anger crosses Fin's eyes. 'Don't fucking say that to me. Don't you *ever* say that.'

'Was my Secret Santa gift from you? The dress?'

His silence answers my question.

'Why?'

'So that you'd be freaked out enough to turn to me. It was supposed to bring us closer together. If you thought someone was accusing you of something then I could be there for you.'

'I don't need anyone to help me,' I say. 'Don't you know that about me?' I glance at the door. There's a chance I could make it, rush to the house and scream for help. But they're all sleeping. Who would hear me? My phone is in my pocket but there's little chance I've got any reception, especially in the garage. I glance at the knife in my hand.

Fin looks at me and frowns. He knows that I won't give up without a fight. He lunges towards me and tries to grab the knife.

I throw myself into him, knocking him off balance, then race towards the door, but Fin's reflexes are too quick and he's right behind me, grabbing my jumper, yanking me backward with such force that I crash to the floor, my knees smashing against the concrete. My scream echoes from the stone walls.

'It doesn't have to be like this,' Fin says.

'Where's Gabby?' I demand, trying to ignore the searing pain in my legs. 'What have you done with her?'

'I took care of everything,' he says, as if it's an achievement to be proud of. 'So you don't have to help with any of that. There's a beautiful loch out there. Vast. No chance of her being found any time soon. Had to search for something to weigh her down, though. Just to make sure she doesn't float up. And soon enough everyone will leave Loch View House and go back to their lives, thinking that Gabby's just cut them off. It wouldn't be the first time she's ghosted us. By the time they find her, any evidence will be washed away. Nothing to trace it to us.' He smiles. 'See, I've taken care of everything for us, Sasha.'

Fin has gone so far now that it's clear there's no way back for him. And that's terrifying. He's already done heinous things to cover his tracks, so I need to tread carefully. My only chance of getting him to tell me everything is to let him believe I will keep quiet. 'Fin, listen. I won't say anything. Ever. I won't talk to the others about this. You can even keep my phone.'

I search his face for any hint that he believes me. I think of Scratch, how heartbroken he'll be if I don't come home, and tears prick my eyes. I have to survive this, for him. And Jarred, too. I didn't give us a chance because I was living in fear of what I might have done, but now I know I didn't hurt Seffie.

There's a long pause, but eventually Fin nods. 'I knew you'd see sense.'

'But first, I need to know what happened to Seffie.'

His eyes narrow.

'Please, Fin. It's the only way I can trust you. And we need to be able to trust each other, don't we, if we stand any chance together?'

Seconds tick by, and a hundred scenarios play out in my head, none of which end well.

'Give me the knife first,' he says, holding out his hand.

With no choice, I hand it to him. And then he opens his mouth to speak, and even before he utters a word, I know I'll never be prepared to hear what happened to that little girl.

TWENTY-EIGHT
BEFORE

Fin stares after Seffie, his heart racing and sweat coating his body. This can't be happening. He won't lose Sasha because of a stupid drunken mistake. He looks at Anna, who only moments ago had been one of his closest friends. But now he loathes the sight of her. He knows it's not just her fault – he didn't have to give in to her just now. But he's in no state to be making good decisions. She'd been so desperate for him, and he's always thought she was sexy. Nothing like Sasha, though. No, to Fin, no woman comes close. 'Go back in the house!' he orders. 'I'll find her. I'll sort this. It will all be okay.'

He leaves Anna crying like a baby, and runs into the woods. Fuck knows where Seffie will be, but he's got to find her before she can get to Sasha.

'Seffie!' he calls. 'Everything's okay. I just need to talk to you. I promise we can sort this all out. Just let me explain. Please.' He forces himself to add that last word, even though he shouldn't have to suck up to this ten-year-old brat. She shouldn't have been following them. Watching them. She's the one who should be apologising to him.

He keeps walking; he can no longer hear the music coming

from the house. 'Seffie? It's not safe for you to be out here. Where are you? Let's go back to the house. Gabby will be wondering where you are.'

Silence. And Fin's cold now, despite still being drenched in sweat. Again, he curses himself. He loves Sasha. He's not going to lose her because of this... this fuck-up. 'Seffie!'

A twig snaps and he stops walking. She's around here somewhere. He calls out to her again, and this time he hears whimpers. She's scared. He can use that to his advantage. 'Seffie, I'm going to tell Sasha the truth. I promise. I made a mistake and I know I don't deserve her. But she's not feeling well. She's gone back to her house. She wasn't even in the garden office when you were hammering on the door. Why don't we both go to see her together and we can talk to her? It will prove to you that I'm being truthful. I made a horrible mistake, Seffie. Please just give me a chance to talk to Sasha. I know how much you care about her. Doesn't she deserve to hear it from me?'

For a moment there's silence, but then Seffie steps out from behind a tree. 'Really?' she says.

Fin holds out his hand. 'Really. Come on, let's get out of this wood. It's giving me the creeps.'

Seffie steps closer to him and looks around. 'Yeah, I think I heard something. Not you. Something else. I'm scared.'

'Then we'd better be quick.'

Fin half expects Seffie to refuse, but she follows him. 'Let's not go back through the house,' he says. 'You don't want Gabby to see you out of bed, do you? I think she's reached her limit, Seffie. I know the way we can go.'

As soon as they're out of the woods, and far enough from Seffie's house, Fin explains the plan. 'Sasha lives too far to walk – she had to get a cab home. But my house is closer. We can grab my car and then drive to Sasha's. Does that sound okay?' He doesn't need to explain that they won't be going to his house at all. Although his parents are likely to still be out, Fin's got the key to his friend Dominic's house, which is close by, so it's better if he takes Seffie there to give him time to think. Fin had been reluctant to look after his friend's cannabis plants while he was away, for fear of Sasha finding out, but now he's glad he gave in and agreed.

Seffie frowns. 'But you've been drinking. It's not safe.'

'I've definitely sobered up now,' Fin says. 'I promise. I would never put you at risk.'

'Okay,' Seffie says, her voice barely audible.

They walk in silence, and Fin's mind whirrs. He doesn't know what the hell he's going to do, but he knows he can't let Seffie tell anyone what happened. He won't lose Sasha – he's waited too long to have her, and finally he's got the chance to be with her. He curses himself for his utter stupidity with Anna. Why the hell had he drunk so much? He's never been good with controlling himself when he's drunk. He knows this. It was all so meaningless – that's the worst part about it.

'There's my house,' Fin says, when they turn into Dominic's road. 'The white one.' He glances at Seffie, who is slowing down now. She could bolt at any second so he needs to be ready.

'Come on,' he says. 'It will all be fine.'

He finds the right key and unlocks the front door. 'I just need to get my car keys,' he says, wondering where Dominic keeps his car keys. He's sure they're in a box in the kitchen.

Seffie hesitates on the porch, glancing around.

'Just come in for a second,' Fin says. 'I have nosy neighbours who'll wonder what a ten-year-old kid is doing up so late.' He ushers her in. Inside, he shuts the door. 'Now, where did I put my keys?'

Without warning, Seffie reaches for the door, trying to yank it open.

'What are you doing?' Fin pulls her back, standing in front of the door.

'I don't believe you! You're not taking me to Sasha, are you?'

The truth is, Fin doesn't know. All he's aware of is that he's cornered. And he needs to do *something*. He can't lose Sasha. He won't lose her.

'This is kidnapping!' Seffie screams. 'Let me go! I'm calling the police!'

'Just calm down!' Fin says, panic flooding through his body. This kid is out of control.

But Seffie ignores him and screams even louder. Ear-piercing shrieks that the neighbours are bound to hear.

'Shut up! Just shut up!'

She won't listen. And now she is lashing out at him, her arms flailing in every direction. Kicking his shins.

He grabs her wrists. 'Fucking stop. And shut up, Seffie!'

'I'm telling the police,' she repeats. 'You've kidnapped me and you'll go to prison.'

That's when he snaps. Everything he's set to lose if Seffie tells the police flashes before him. Sasha. His career. He's going to make something of himself, and he can't let Seffie ruin that. Grabbing her neck, he grips tightly and shakes her, as if she's a ragdoll. She's so light, he can barely feel her weight, and is hardly aware of what he's doing.

'I told you to stop!' he says. 'Just bloody stop!'

But she won't stop, and even though he's got hold of her neck, she still kicks out, trying her best to fight back.

No longer in control of himself, Fin squeezes harder, until eventually the kicking stops and everything falls silent.

TWENTY-NINE

NOW

02:32

An avalanche of tears floods down my face when Fin finishes speaking. He, though, is emotionless, recounting what he did to Seffie as if he was telling me details of a film he's watched. Cold. Detached. How can this be the same man I loved? It's clear that he's not, though. What he did to Seffie changed him, turned him into something monstrous.

Nausea floods through my body like a tidal wave, but I need to keep it together if I'm to have any chance of getting out of this alive.

'It was quick,' Fin says. 'Seffie didn't suffer too much.'

His words just confirm to me how unstable he is. 'You slept with Anna. All of this happened because of that.' I think of what happened with Shaun, but there's a world of difference.

'I'm sorry I did that to you,' he says. 'When the whole time you were waiting for me.'

But I don't care about that. If I'd known at the time it would have shaken me to my core, but now it barely has an impact.

'Does Anna know what you did to Seffie?' I struggle to understand why she wouldn't say anything.

'All this time I thought she believed me when I told her I couldn't find Seffie in the woods,' Fin says.

'But she knew Seffie went into the woods and you chased after her? She must have known it was you.'

'When we have to, Sasha, we can make any lie sound like the truth. Who knows what's going on in Anna's head? She felt so guilty about what we'd done that she wanted to believe me. And I told her whatever I needed to so that she'd be convinced. She didn't want to think that her actions might have caused Seffie's disappearance. So of course she didn't say anything, otherwise it would have all come out. If you think about it, we're all culpable in some way, aren't we? And you were the one who was supposed to be looking out for Seffie. Anyway, no point dwelling on that now. I think we have a problem with Anna. Maybe she's been thinking it all over and now she's ready to talk about what we did. Now do you see why we have to stick together? Find out if she sent Gabby that email.'

Having read Anna's letter to Gabby, it seems very likely to me that it was Anna. My stomach clenches and a chill runs through my body. 'Why did you have to kill Gabby? All she wanted was to know what happened to Seffie.'

'No. She wanted justice. Gabby would never have let it go,' Fin says, 'and eventually, when she realised it wasn't you, she would have found out what I'd done.'

I can't look at him.

'You didn't have to—'

'I did it for you! For *us*! How many times do I have to tell you that? I would have lost you forever if it all came out. I couldn't have that. This was all Seffie's fault. If she hadn't been creeping around, spying on people the whole night. If she'd just stayed in her bloody room.'

'Don't you dare blame her!' I shout. 'You chose to sleep with Anna!'

'It was a drunken mistake. I loved *you*, Sasha. That's why I couldn't let Seffie tell you. I didn't want to lose you.'

'But you still lost me. There would never have been a way back for us. And Seffie lost her life for nothing.' I swipe at relentless tears. 'What... what did you do with... with Seffie?'

Fin hesitates. Maybe this is the end of the line, where he stops talking. Which means I have run out of time.

But this time Fin's surprisingly willing to talk. 'I kept her in the boot of Dominic's car,' he says. 'Even if Dominic had found anything suspicious, he was the last person who'd contact the police, not with his illegal cannabis farm. And the next day I drove as far as I could in the middle of the night. To a railway track. There was a huge verge where no one would ever go. Seffie's buried there.'

I need him to stop; I don't want this picture of poor Seffie in my head. It's bad enough that I know the things I already do. 'I'm sorry this happened to you,' I lie. 'It must have been so hard for you.' I glance at the knife in his hand; there's no way I'll be able to prise it from him.

Fin frowns. 'Yeah. It was hard. I didn't want anyone to die. None of this was supposed to happen.'

'You did what you had to do,' I say. 'You had no choice.'

Slowly, he nods. The fact that he is willing to believe me shows just how deranged his mind is. 'Yeah, yeah, I did.'

I crawl closer to him. 'You know, I would have done exactly the same. If I'd been you.' The words slice into my throat.

He smiles. 'I know what you're doing,' he says. 'And it won't work. You've never been a good liar, have you?'

I spring up, rushing towards the shelves at the back of the garage, where the tools are the only chance I have. Again, Fin reacts quickly, and I feel him right behind me, his hand reaching for me. 'You bitch,' he says. 'Liar! Now you've left me with no choice.' I dart sideways. I'm almost there – the hammer's within reaching distance. But I feel Fin tugging at my clothes. I'm no match for his strength. I picture Seffie, dancing to 'All I Want For Christmas' in her silver sequinned dress. The joy on her face. With one final effort, I grab the hammer, my fingers gripping it just as Fin drags me down. With all my strength, I spin around, swinging the hammer, smashing it into his face.

There's a heavy thud, followed by a scream, and I'm not sure if it's my own or not. I'm crashing to the ground, my head thudding on the concrete.

Fin, too, lies on the floor, clutching his head, bright red blood fanning around him. I pull myself up and reach into his pocket, grabbing my phone, praying for a signal. There's one bar on my phone.

'No,' he gasps, clutching my arm. 'Let me die. Please. Just let me die, Sash.'

If Fin had truly loved me, then this might be an impossible decision to make. But it was never about love. It was fixation. Obsession. Or something else I will never understand.

I pull free of his grip, and dial 999.

And after speaking to the police, I call Anna and ask her to tell everyone to come to the garage. With no telling when the police will be able to get here, the rest of us need to stick together now.

Just like it should have always been.

A LETTER FROM KATHRYN

Dear Reader,

Thank you so much for choosing to read *The Christmas Party*. It was initially an Audible Original and I'm thrilled that it's now also available in ebook and paperback. This is the first novella I've written, and although shorter than my usual novels, it definitely challenged me and pushed me out of my comfort zone.

I really hope you enjoyed it, and if you did, I'd be very grateful if you could write a review. I'd love to hear what you think and it also helps new readers discover my books.

If you'd like to keep up to date with all my latest releases, just sign up at the following link. Your email address will never be shared and you can unsubscribe at any time.

www.bookouture.com/kathryn-croft

I love hearing from my readers, so please do get in touch through social media or my website.

Thanks so much!

Kathryn

KEEP IN TOUCH WITH KATHRYN

www.kathryncroft.com

- facebook.com/authorkathryncroft
- instagram.com/authorkathryncroft
- x.com/katcroft

ACKNOWLEDGEMENTS

There are so many people I'm grateful to for making *The Christmas Party*, my first novella and Audible Original, happen. It was a real challenge to condense a story and plot into half the words of a full-length novel, and I had many sleepless nights where I wondered if I could actually do it! Not to mention the tightest deadline I've ever known!

But anyway, it happened and it's all thanks to the following wonderful people:

Robin Morgan-Bentley – thank you for commissioning me to write this novella for Audible. It was an honour to be selected and thank you for your belief and faith in me.

Hannah Todd – thank you for championing me when I didn't think I could do it (and when I completely changed the initial idea, leaving me even less time to finish it!)

Billie Piper and Avita Jay – I have so much gratitude to you both for narrating this book so beautifully, and not just narrating it but *performing* the words and bringing this story to life.

Lydia Vassar-Smith – thank you for taking this novella on for Bookouture in ebook and paperback formats, I'm overwhelmed by your faith in me.

Bill Massey, Miranda Ward and Jenni Davis – thank you for all your Audible editorial input which knocked this book into much better shape.

Jenny Page – thank you for your Bookouture editorial input – it's much appreciated.

Jo Sidaway and Michelle Langford – thanks again for your police procedural insights – always a pleasure discussing where someone could hide a body!

RAISING READERS
Books Build Bright Futures

Dear Reader,

We'd love your attention for one more page to tell you about the crisis in children's reading, and what we can all do.

Studies have shown that reading for fun is the **single biggest predictor of a child's future life chances** – more than family circumstance, parents' educational background or income. It improves academic results, mental health, wealth, communication skills, ambition and happiness.

The number of children reading for fun is in rapid decline. Young people have a lot of competition for their time, and a worryingly high number do not have a single book at home.

Hachette works extensively with schools, libraries and literacy charities, but here are some ways we can all raise more readers:

- Reading to children for just 10 minutes a day makes a difference
- Don't give up if children aren't regular readers – there will be books for them!

- Visit bookshops and libraries to get recommendations
- Encourage them to listen to audiobooks
- Support school libraries
- Give books as gifts

There's a lot more information about how to encourage children to read on our websites: **www.RaisingReaders.co.uk** and **www.JoinRaisingReaders.com**.

Thank you for reading.